101 BUR

MW01103923

Beyond the
PASSION

A Novel

Brian Buriff

Inmate Na~
IDOC #
Prov~
Aut~
~
us Trujillo:

Evergreen
PRESS

Beyond the Passion by Brian Buriff
Copyright © 2005 by Brian Buriff

All rights reserved. No portion of this publication may be re-produced, stored in a retrieval system, or transmitted in any form or by any means, electronic, mechanical, photocopy, recording, or otherwise, without the written permission of the author, except as provided by US copyright law. All Scripture citations are from the King James Version of the Bible.

Printed and bound in the United States of America
For worldwide distribution

First Printing 2005

ISBN 1-58169-180-7

Evergreen Press
P.O. 191540
Mobile AL 36619
(800) 367-8203

Dedication

To my wife, Amber, with love

Acknowledgments

This novel has been an ever-evolving project with so many friends who have inspired and encouraged me. I am grateful to my son Cody, for the hours of artistic creativity he invested during the concept phase. Although your earliest designs for a book cover were never used in the finished product, they were absolutely eye-catching and gave me the vision to believe that this was a novel that could potentially stand out on store shelves.

My hat is also off to Linda Hauser who, once again, did not spare her masterful red-ink pen of editorial correction on the earlier manuscript drafts.

For being a friend and a silent prayer partner, I am grateful to Paul Murphy.

For going the extra mile and constructively coaching this manuscript forward, I am grateful to Keith Carroll.

And to the good people at Evergreen Press—for working patiently with me and providing the tools to make this novel available to the wider public—you have my gratitude.

Most especially, I am grateful to my wife, my sons, and countless others who have encouraged me in this project.

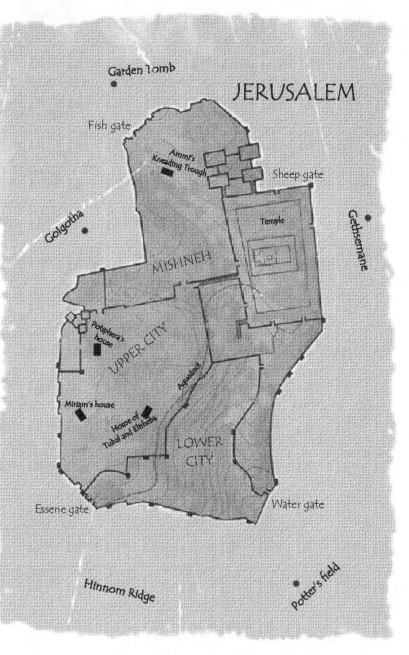

Garden Tomb

JERUSALEM

Fish gate

Ammi's
Kneading Trough

Sheep gate

Golgotha

Temple

Gethsemane

MISHNEH

Potiphera's
house

UPPER CITY

Miriam's house

Aqueduct

House of
Tubal and Elisheba

LOWER
CITY

Essene gate

Water gate

Hinnom Ridge

Potter's field

Character Notes

Characters in the Bible frequently shared identical names, which is sometimes confusing to modern readers. For instance, there is more than one Mary and Joseph in the Bible. To distinguish between the characters, this novel uses Jewish, Roman and derivatives of other names so that no two names are alike, hopefully making for an easier read.

Miriam
The Hebrew name for Mary. In this novel, Miriam is the Mary whose house in Jerusalem was the common gathering place for the disciples (Acts 12:12). She is not to be confused with Mary the mother of Jesus or Mary from Bethany, sister of Martha and Lazarus.

Magdalene
An abbreviation for Mary Magdalene or Mary of Magdala, first noticed in Luke 8:2.

Maria
She was that "other Mary" who was present at the burial of our Lord (Mark 15:47).

Marcus
Referred to in Scripture as "John, whose surname was Mark" (Acts 12:12, 25). Marcus was his Roman name, which gradually came to supersede his Jewish name, John.

Yoseph
The Hebrew name for Joseph. In this novel, Yoseph is Joseph of Arimathea, a secret disciple of Jesus (Mark 15:43). He is not to be confused with Joseph the son of Jacob, or Joseph the foster-father of Jesus.

Simeon

The elongated form of the name Simon. In this novel, Simeon is the father of Judas Iscariot (John 6:71). This Simeon is not to be confused with the temple prophet at our Lord's birth, or the disciple Simon Peter, who appears in this book under the name Peter.

Introduction

Concerning the hours and days spanning the crucifixion and resurrection of Christ, many essays, books, and sermons have explored what may have transpired in the metaphysical, heavenly abodes. However, very few books have ventured into what may have transpired on the human platform.

Undoubtedly, in the wake of Christ's Passion, a multi-layered drama quickly unfolded on different stages involving a cast of human characters—the disciples and the women—each of whom was probably very raw in his emotions and colorful in his responses to unimaginable crises. With all hope gone, it's difficult to believe that everything was neat and tidy. Rather, these were real people with real feelings dealing with a real series of tragic events.

This novel is about the painful, but necessary, expressions of shock and sorrow, blaming and bargaining, and the illusions and disillusionment that are part of the grief process. Like a butterfly emerging from its cocoon, the disciples and women whom Jesus loved found themselves contending with the wrappings of doubt and fear that enveloped them. To deny their pain and struggle is to ignore an integral process that was necessary for their wings to find strength and take flight in the wake of the coming resurrection.

Beyond the Passion engages the curious in the human drama bridging the death and resurrection of Christ. It's a fictitious probe into questions such as, "Who found Judas' corpse?" "What was his funeral like?" "Concerning Peter, where did he go after the denial?" And, "How was he reconciled in time to join the post-Sabbath excursion to the empty tomb?"

In the pages that follow, step inside the skin of the men and women of Christ's Passion. See their pain. Feel their sufferings. And find their hope.

You may recognize yourself in them, want to be like them,

or want to hate them. As you experience the temptations and tests of each, you may gradually find it safer to acknowledge your own darker side, without which you could not fully appreciate the hope and inspiration of grace that makes this story possible. In the final analysis, you may even come to agree that the absence of detail within that 40-hour span between the crucifixion and resurrection may really be an act of charity, offering grace to a cast of characters who, in so many ways, are simply a mirrored reflection of our own lives today.

—*Brian Buriff, 2005*

ONE

The tangled cord would suffice. It was old and frayed, perhaps once used as a halter to lead an ox to graze or a bull to the temple for sacrifice. The best ropes were made of goat or camel hair. These strands were woven of flax—first spun into threads and then twisted and plaited into a cord. Its length was sufficient for a man who was suffocating in despair. Hugging the shadows, the lone figure ambled away from Jerusalem, methodically untangling the knotted rope as feelings of guilt and paranoia swept over him.

A short time earlier, Judas had paid what would be his last visit to the house of Tubal and Elishaba. These faithful friends were generous in their hospitality. Each year, they opened their home to his aging father and mother for lodging during the Passover. Without detection, Judas had quietly entered his parents' room. On a wooden table next to his mother's bed, he placed the brass ring his father had given him 11 years earlier—a token of favor, dignity, and affection—and quickly left.

The ring had once been worn on the fourth finger of his left hand. The ancients believed that a vein ran from that finger directly to the heart. But today his heart was shredded. Favor no longer ran through his blood. Dignity no longer befitted this once chosen student of the Messiah. His lineage had become his curse.

Judas, surnamed Iscariot, native of Kerioth, was the son of Simeon and Ruhamah. Only three years earlier the Nazarene had handpicked Judas, and he followed Him with zeal. This Messiah was the Promised One, anointed to deliver the Jews—invincible, all-powerful, and capable of wielding heaven's mighty sword to destroy every enemy of Yahweh God.

In Judea, 10 miles south of Hebron, the villagers of the closely neighboring hamlets of Kerioth-Hezron could not have been more proud that the Teacher had selected their short but handsome native son. Over the years, they had watched young Judas grow up in their fortified, little frontier village. His family tended their livestock on the pastoral plains of the Negeb. To forge a living in this region was a difficult burden, only made harder by the oppressive taxation of Rome.

What Judas lacked in stature he more than made up for in courage. More than once Judas stood up to the intimidation of the tax collectors by outsmarting them—sometimes in ways that were less than principled. Now, under this Messiah, there was hope for enduring change, and Judas was sure he would be at the center of any political shake-up.

Other Keriothians found Judas' sudden departure to be disconcerting. "Has he gone mad?" the people whispered. "Can the Teacher really depend on that impulsive young man?" They knew that Judas was apt to bounce from cause to cause, and had difficulty staying focused on any one thing.

Still, his parents had undoubtedly taken enormous pride in him. Named after the tribe of Judah, his name meant "the praise of Yahweh." He was their firstborn and great delight. With such pride, however, came enormous pressure. Simeon made it unmistakably clear that he had high expectations for his son. Eking out a life on the harsh Judean frontier was tough work. Failure was not an option. While the livestock grazed, Simeon flew into a tirade if Judas was even marginally distracted from his work.

Forcefully, he once yanked his son over to a barren fig tree and ranted, "You're no better than this tree! What do you have to show for yourself? Trees like this are worth nothing and are cut down. Is that what you want for yourself? Work harder, Judas! Stay focused on your task!"

Reflecting on his earliest boyhood memories, Judas recalled a time when he accidentally fell down and scraped a knee.

"Whimpering?" his father had mocked. "Keriothians don't cry! Be a man!"

Judas' father was seemingly void of all compassion and insisted that his son get up immediately that day and return to his chores. On those rare occasions when Ruhamah jumped in to defend her son, Simeon just shrugged and said, "What is that to me?"

For Judas, growing up in a pastoral home sometimes meant barely having enough to eat. He once was sent to bed still hungry after eating a meager meal of boiled rice. Afraid to pester his father, Judas went to Ruhamah who, with the tender love of a mother, gave him a small roll of parched bread. She told him not to eat it, but to hold it. And if he held it through the night, there would always be enough bread for tomorrow. With that little morsel of security, the boy drifted off to sleep, his hands wrapped around the bread.

As Judas progressed through adolescence and into early manhood, he became increasingly plagued by feelings of insecurity and insignificance, and felt tremendous pressure to be perfect. But now that the Nazarene had chosen him, he thought, perhaps this was his chance to really become someone—to make a difference and to live up to his name.

No wonder the Messiah had delegated to him the responsibilities of handling the group's money, thought Judas. He knew he could be trusted to care for it, to guard it day and night, ensuring that there would always be enough bread for tomorrow.

But when Judas had arisen on this Jerusalem morning, toward the end of an especially long Passover week, the bread was gone, consumed by his own betrayal. His quest to untangle the mess he had created the night before still yielded nothing. Hope was deadlocked, his iniquity too great.

And the rope? It was far too convenient.

To be cast at the devil's mercy now seemed to be the only clear path.

UNDER THE unbearable load of his guilt, Judas now lumbered along the rocky path near the base of the Hinnom ridge. There, he stopped and gazed southward and up high toward his destination.

Don't they see what harm they've done? Mother, I really did try. Father, you know I wanted to please you as well, but I just couldn't live up to your standards. Couldn't you see how scared I was of you? I was always on edge, waiting for the next assault. Just as I was afraid of never having enough, I was equally afraid of never being enough.

Mother, thank you for the bread. Thank you for the times you tried to rescue me. But my hunger was for more than mere bread. The devil consumed every morsel of confidence I had.

Why didn't Jesus see this flaw in me? He must have known. Why did He pick me? Why didn't He help me? Maybe He does deserve to die. I certainly do.

Climbing ever higher toward the precipice, Judas knew that very few people would ever truly understand the reasons behind his betrayal. He knew that fear, rather than greed, had motivated the terrible deed.

I was desperate. I thought it was worth the gamble. Jesus wasn't supposed to be taken. Couldn't He deliver Himself? Just who failed whom last night?

Indeed, Jesus had known what was coming. He told Judas to make haste. In hindsight, Judas rationalized that if only Jesus had come through on His end, they would've had all the money they needed to sustain the work. That would show those religious leaders! The last laugh was supposed to be on them. No harm done. Right?

But his excuses weren't good enough. His rationalizations were insufficient to pardon his vexed mind. *How could I have been so wrong?*

STANDING ATOP the Hinnom ridge, the view of Jerusalem was breathtaking. The shadows were receding from the western wall of the great city. The streets below had sprung to life.

The Sabbath was coming, and the townspeople were bustling about in preparation for the prescribed sacred rest. Centuries before, the petty injunctions of the religious leaders had converted this day of joy into an intolerable burden.

Still, for some, this day was happily anticipated. When the head of the household returned to his family on the Sabbath-eve, he would often find his home festively adorned. That evening, the blessings of Israel would be imparted upon each child. On the Sabbath, even the stranger, the poor, and the widow were remembered.

As Judas observed the activity of the townspeople and venders down below, he noticed that the commotion near the palace of the Roman procurator, Pontius Pilate, had subsided. The remaining guards and townspeople still congregating were now slowly moving toward the northwest sector.

Unraveling the final knot from his cord, Judas looked straight down into the deep, narrow ravine separating the mountain city from its dumping ground. Its steep, rocky sides had been difficult for Judas to traverse. Except for a few trees at the top, it was mostly covered with rocks and low, woody shrubs. Appropriately, it was nicknamed the "Hill of Evil Counsel."

To the Jews, Hinnom was synonymous with hell. It was the place of the damned. According to ancient records, King

Solomon erected high places on this ridge to the pagan god Molech. At a particular location called Tophet, or the "fire-stove," Kings Ahaz and Manasseh made their children "pass through the fire." Innocent children were sacrificed to the fire gods in this fiendish custom.

Last night I also sacrificed innocence, moaned Judas.

The Nazarene was guilty of nothing, yet Judas could look down and see Him being herded through a Jerusalem alley like a murderous felon.

Am I not the murderer? Long ago, my own innocence ended. I'm the one who was wrong. Why couldn't they see that? Take me, not Him!

Atop the ridge, Judas studied one of the older redbud trees—about 30 feet tall—that had a large branch overhanging the precipice. It was late spring and the purple-red blossoms had progressively yielded to the dark green, heart-shaped leaves.

On its backside away from the precipice, a low branch provided a good foothold by which Judas climbed up into the tree. Down below he could see the rocky pavement. *Don't look down,* Judas chided himself. *You'll get dizzy and blunder this, too.*

With the rope in hand, he climbed higher and then scooted out onto a far limb. Trembling, afraid of falling, Judas tested its sturdiness. *Why should I be scared?* he thought. Fear had driven him to do everything else he'd done the last nine hours. *Why should I let it stop me now?*

Cautiously, he stretched out farther onto the limb and secured the rope to the branch with a sturdy knot.

Down below, he could clearly see the sewage and debris from the dump. To put an end to the horrid abomination of child sacrifice, King Josiah had deliberately polluted the area. He rendered it ceremonially unclean by spreading it with human bones and other corruptions. From that time forward, it became the city's garbage dump, where all refuse and human waste were deposited.

This is where I deserve to die, a place where innocence died, a dumping ground for garbage and human sewage, he told himself. *Yet, I'm so afraid.*

Judas' mind was whirling. He felt he was suffocating with the weight of his own shame; yet he was still grasping for one last ray of hope.

What should it matter if it hurts? He tried to reason with himself. *Life, itself, already hurts too badly. To die and get it over with is the better choice, my only choice.*

Easing back toward the safety of the tree's center, Judas shed his outer garment. The cloak dropped and landed silently at the base of the tree. It was in stark contrast to the memory of the harsh clanking of silver coins that had landed at the feet of the priests.

Why couldn't they have just taken their money back? Was that too much to ask? I threw it all down. I hurled all of it at their feet. I didn't keep any of it. It wasn't that much. Indeed, 30 silver pieces amounted to no more than the fair market value of a slave.

Just what kind of priests are they, anyhow? When I returned the money and confessed my guilt, they smugly said, 'What is that to us?' And then they walked away. That's what my father used to say and do. Couldn't they have said something else? Has NOTHING changed? Just when I needed the representatives of Yahweh most, they let me down. They are priests of the devil!

Slowly, Judas looped the rope and tied a loose knot at the end, testing it to be sure it would easily slide. He had tied this knot thousands of times before when he worked on the Negeb plain, but this time it was for him alone.

Holding the rope up and ducking his head forward, Judas slid the ligature around his neck. The coarse weave of the rope first scraped against the underside of his chin and then dropped lower near his shoulders, the knot to one side. Reaching his arms up to the side of his head, Judas slipped the knot down so that the cord lifted back up under his chin, snug against his jawbone. This rope that once led animals to the temple sacrifice would now lead him to his own sacrifice. His reproach required punishment. His pain required relief. This was the cord of atonement.

Still agonizing over what might have been, Judas gazed back at the city. There he could make out the scene—three prisoners were struggling along a road, each carrying a horizontal crossbeam.

On a distant ridge just outside the Jerusalem walls, next to a thoroughfare, another crowd seemed to be gathering. That ridge consisted of a rounded knoll that had a skull-like appearance in its southern portion. It was the place of execution. From where Judas was perched, he could see two of the five vertical posts still in place from the executions earlier that week.

Crucifixion was reserved for slaves and villains of the worst class. The condemned were forced to carry their own wooden crosses up the ridge to where they would experience the most frightful of sufferings. Sometimes the soldiers mercifully shortened the agony of the crucified by breaking their legs, lighting fires under their crosses, or unleashing wild beasts on them. Other times, the condemned would linger for as much as two or three days, until they finally succumbed to suffocation, dehydration, or starvation.

Today, the distant ridge would play host to another round of executions. Three of the five cross posts had been taken down to be recycled for the torture. The two that remained on the hill stood upright and empty. From afar, they appeared as harmless as little toy sticks. Up close, however, there was no mistaking their intent.

Judas knew that his father and mother were probably

preparing for the Sabbath. His mother was sure to have already found the ring. However, they would have no idea where their son was, and no idea of the danger he was in. Two days earlier, he had overheard his parents bragging that he was the treasurer for the Messiah, the coming King. Power would belong to their son! Position and prestige would be his. Finally, they could be proud of their son. "That's our boy. We knew he wouldn't fail!"

From a distant place in his mind, however, he could hear the devils screaming, "But you have failed!"

Of course, I have failed.

"You've ruined everything!"

Stop torturing me! I know this already.

Too weary to cry any more, Judas succumbed to one final internal beating.

"You've let everyone down! You've shattered everyone's expectations! Judas, you are accursed!" the devils screamed.

From his perch high atop the Hill of Evil Counsel, Judas could almost hear a dull murmuring coming from the distant rocks as if they, too, had chimed in on the chorus of condemnation. "You didn't produce any fruit," they seemed to moan, "but I was patient. I dug around you. I fertilized you. I kept you growing. And after awhile, I looked. But there was still no fruit, so I cut you down."

Straddling the branch, Judas raised his right leg up and rested his knee on the branch. Precariously balanced, he felt the coarse bark against his knee pressing into his trembling hands. Sweat beaded on his forehead and dripped down his neck as he contemplated just how to make the release.

As if the world was slowly pulling away from him, everything now seemed to grow strangely quiet. A pigeon high above him in the uppermost branches could only be seen, not heard. While it frantically opened and closed its beak, chirping its song, there was no sound. It was as if the bird was mute or

Judas had suddenly gone deaf. The outside world seemed to move at a slow, dreamy tempo.

From deep within he cried out, fighting against his pain, still hoping to be heard. But he was no longer able to even hear himself. *Hold on*, Judas pressed. *Just listen. Perhaps. . .*

Even the air itself had grown totally silent—there was not even a breeze. He groped for something, anything, to cry back to him, but the chasm was too great. Except for the faint, arduous pounding of his heartbeat and the deep, ragged gasp of his breath, Judas could hear nothing. The silence was deafening.

Perched and ready for the release, death could no longer be resisted. Oblivion now beckoned, more desirable than the pain of living. Only from the abyss of despair did Judas sense any response to his final plea to live. It was the final mocking of the devils: "What is that to us!"

THE SUDDEN plunge was quickly interrupted by the abrupt snap of Judas' neck. The extreme force threw his head sideways in a violent whiplash. Cervical vertebrae fractured. Intervertebral disks tore. Nerve roots stripped. Ligaments popped. Muscles stretched beyond their ability to flex. Spasms of scapular and shoulder pain radiated from the spinal cord. Friction from the coarse weave of the cord burned against his ear.

The body of Judas Iscariot now yo-yoed spastically from the rope, twisting from side to side, completely suspended over the precipice. But he was still alive.

The branch from which he dangled vaulted and arched, creaking under the sudden strain. Blossoms shook loose, falling gently. Leaves, shredded and stripped, grazed by the rope, seesawed as they floated downward.

Beneath his chin, Judas felt the sudden constriction of his

airway. His trachea collapsed. His esophagus kinked. Gasping. Choking. Writhing.

The strangulation of air to his lungs mated with the occlusion of major blood vessels in his throat and neck. During brief moments of ebbing consciousness, a feverish acidic burn scorched upward through his head as carotid arteries and jugular veins compressed.

Writhing in the air, Judas frantically reached below his chin to pull at the rope. There was no relief. The upward cinch of the cord was unyielding in its death grip. His arms and hands tingled—weakening; his legs were flailing in the air.

Blood and saliva quickly pooled in his throat.

Fear. Panic.

Above the ligature, veins swelled and arteries engorged.

His head was stinging; his extremities were throbbing.

Stop this! Reverse the gruesome madness! But it was too late.

His skin was already ashen. Strangulation was winning. The violent thrashing of his legs diminished and the pendulous wrenching of his torso waned. Feebly, his fingers clawed the air. His eyes remained wide-open, fixated and marbled—resisting the curtain of darkness that was slowly descending. Air was all around him, but unsuccessful in its struggle for a way in.

Spurts of fight slowly twitched away. Involuntary quivering recessed. Lifelessly, barely swaying now, his body dangled. His arms went limp, dead to his side.

Just seconds before, during his last crack of tormented consciousness, Judas had gazed out toward the city and beheld the mob in the far northwest sector. In his final blurry glimpse, before drifting into the black, he noticed that one of the condemned prisoners—the last in the procession—had just stumbled and fallen to the ground.

11

TWO

The thoroughfare leading back into the city was already less crowded. Those returning home from the bloody matinee didn't leave disappointed. Jerusalem didn't have coliseums, gladiators or lions, but she sure had Golgotha—the place of the skull!

Yoseph didn't make it to the executions today. Instead, the aging religious leader was delayed by urgent government business. Dealing with the Judean magistrates, particularly with the jurisdictional overlaps between Roman and Jewish authorities, could leave one flustered. However, Yoseph was as patient as he was resourceful. He was familiar with the bureaucrats and knew with whom he needed to confer to expedite his request. Once everything was signed and officially sealed, Yoseph hastened from the city, documents in hand, up toward Golgotha.

His trek toward the execution site was oddly conspicuous. To others, it looked as though he was traveling the wrong way. The show was already over. Although the tide was thinning, he was still awkwardly trudging against the cumbersome flow of the crowd.

Yoseph further stood out because of his religious robes, which, in his haste, he had forgotten to shed. Wearing the long, flowing garments of the Sanhedrin office was helpful in pressing for the earlier meeting with the procurator, but now they were uncomfortable and signaled to this mixed crowd his role in the crucifixion events.

Those who deplored the executions protested to Yoseph and scoffed at him as they passed. Others, who had savored the bloody amusement, crowed their approval.

Coming from the site, one young fellow hollered, "Better hurry—they just smashed the knees!" Around him, his friends, carefree and highly animated, imitated the gasps and bellows that had entertained them just minutes before. As the young bucks guffawed down the road, the young man turned back and followed Yoseph.

"Why are you going up there now?" he asked, inspecting Yoseph's stately garments.

"This has nothing to do with you!" Yoseph barked at him.

"You do know that it's over, don't you? You're too late."

"Go on, now!" Yoseph waved him away, irritated.

As Yoseph continued on his journey, alone again, he was reminded of why he detested this place. Against the backdrop of a prodigious and majestic city was this hideous little knoll. Earlier when the sun had mysteriously darkened and the landscape was devoid of its usual earthen hues, the hill took on an ominous appearance.

Now, just after the sixth hour, daylight was returning, but the sun was sitting low in the sky. Deep shadows cast across the southern face of Golgotha accentuated the rocky crannies that resembled eye sockets and cheekbones on a bare skull. Between the hill's appearance and the executions atop, this whole area appeared dark and morbid.

On his approach, Yoseph saw that the torturous exhibition was indeed over. It was halted earlier than usual. Often the corpses were left dangling for days, but this was Preparation Day, and the Jews didn't want the bodies still hanging during the Sabbath.

To hasten their deaths, attending soldiers had clubbed the legs and kneecaps of two of the crucified men. The men screamed and writhed in pain. Some onlookers grimaced while others cheered and applauded.

Unable to push themselves upright with their legs to relieve the pressure on their arms and wrists, the crucified men slumped under their own weight, putting unbearable stress on their ribs and lungs. Every breath became laborious as upper abdominal tissues and chest muscles stretched and tore. Bloody saliva gurgled in their airways and eventually suffocation stole its prisoners.

Enthralled with the process of shattering bone and cartilage, the guards would have started in on the third prisoner had the attending centurion not stepped in. He informed them that this prisoner was already dead. He was the one some had called the "King of the Jews."

To certify death, the brawny, well-tanned centurion reached up and poked his spear under the arms and around the ribs of the man. There was no response. When most of the crowd disbanded and the women were not looking, he quickly punctured the side of the prisoner, just under the ribs. A gelatinized mixture of serum and congealed blood oozed from the man's diaphragm.

By the time Yoseph arrived, the first body was already being pulled down from its cross. Since no one was there to claim this body, the attending guards exercised little care as they roughly yanked it off and allowed it to fall limply to the ground.

Once the corpse was laid out on the stretcher and the guards began freeing the second body, Yoseph approached the attending centurion. Yoseph couldn't help but notice this warrior's muscular forearms protruding from his armor. He was the commander of his regiment, in charge of 100 fighting men.

The customary duties of a centurion included drilling his

men, inspecting their armament, supervising their food and clothing, and commanding them in the field. Centurions were chosen by merit and were known for their courage, constancy and strength of mind.

As stout as this centurion was, however, something seemed oddly different about his demeanor. He didn't exhibit the gory passion that normally accompanied his job. In fact, his eyes were bloodshot and shifting. The commander seemed to have lost his focus. Something had jarred him.

Most of the Roman contingent had already been sent back to their barracks. The guards who remained were ordered to forgo the normal jesting and joking that often happened in the aftermath of public executions.

When Yoseph drew near, the centurion jerked to attention, quickly raising his spear.

"Back off!" the centurion barked, now vigilant.

"Pardon my intrusion," said Yoseph, "but I have—"

"No!" A scream suddenly pierced the air.

Yoseph barely caught a glimpse of the person who barreled toward him, knocking him down. Falling sideways, Yoseph gasped for air as the wind was knocked out of him. First one blow and then another rained down on his nose and jaw.

The fists that pummeled his face were those of a thin 22-year-old woman. It was Magdalene, one of the young maidens who attended to the mother of Jesus. While slender and usually delicate in manner, the scowl on her face radiated the fury of a hundred Roman warriors.

"How could you do this!" she yelled, with a blood-curdling cry. "You killed Him!"

Moments earlier, Magdalene had watched as Yoseph approached from a distance. She didn't know him personally, but she recognized the garb of a Sanhedrin officer—an executive from the religious body that had orchestrated this mutilation.

Magdalene had restrained herself earlier in the day for fear of the religious officials and what they might do. But this official had the gall to just stroll up to the execution site alone.

This is my chance, she had thought. And then she raced toward the man.

IT HAD been eight months since Magdalene had lashed out and attacked someone like this. Before meeting the Nazarene, she had been much more aggressive and unpredictable.

Magdalene was originally from the small, obscure village of Dalmanutha—located on the western shore of the Tiberius Lake. Dalmanutha, known as the "the city of color," was where indigo plants were widely cultivated. Magdalene had lived in the district called "The Tower of Dyers."

Her personality was as colorful and vibrant as the business of her aunt and uncle, with whom she had lived. For the most part, she was lively and outgoing. On some occasions, however, Magdalene had suffered from dark mood swings and even seizures, all of which were attributed to demonic influences. Her fiendish spells were marked by a level of verbal and physical aggression that caused even the local priests to shudder.

When the Nazarene met her, she was engulfed in her most hair-raising episode yet. Witnesses reported that she spoke in a myriad of voices, perhaps as many as seven, and verbally attacked the Nazarene.

Instead of turning away from her, however, the Nazarene had reached toward her—even as she violently batted Him away. When He called the sickness out of her, she slumped to the ground and lay motionless. Eventually she awakened—confused but no longer in need of restraints.

Months of good health followed. Magdalene learned to cherish each new day of freedom and growth. It became easier for her to break old habits and cultivate new ways of thinking. During her darkest years, her foibles had served as a crutch upon which she depended heavily to help her survive. But now, they were no longer needed. She was free! Only on certain occasions did she doubt her progress and wonder if her mind was really purged of the old voices that had once vexed her.

AS MAGDALENE continued beating the man, she felt energized by the awareness that she was still in her right mind. She knew what she was doing. Her mind was not clouded. Her indignation was pure, righteous, and free of any demonic influence.

By virtue of serving on the Sanhedrin, Yoseph had not only misjudged and failed the Nazarene, he also represented everything Magdalene resented about the priests from Dalmanutha, who had misjudged and failed her. Eight months before, whenever she turned violent, she would have no recollection of the episodes; but today, she was in her right mind. She knew exactly what was happening and why she was doing it. She could actually feel her cold fists striking the pallid, doughy face of the intruder.

Strangely enough, Yoseph did not resist the assault. While he attempted to cover his face, he made very little effort to push her away. Had it not been for the centurion who yanked her off, Magdalene would have continued to pummel him.

As Yoseph rolled over on his side, he could see the centurion holding the disheveled Magdalene, kicking and cursing wildly in his arms. Lifting himself to his knees, he paused to rest. Then he planted his foot on the ground to get up.

Suddenly, Yoseph grimaced in pain as his ribs were kicked violently, and he fell back to the ground. Once again, Yoseph was at the mercy of an enraged woman—but it was a different one this time!

THE HANDS that attacked Yoseph this time were not the closed fists of young Magdalene, but the open hands and fingers of a much older, yet equally tenacious, woman. They slapped at the sides of his face and across his neck. This woman had the longer fingernails of someone refined and privileged, of someone who didn't engage in menial labor that would otherwise require short, stubby nails.

Miriam took her turn hitting the man. Strong and outspoken, she had been a wealthy supporter of the Nazarene and a best friend to His mother. Both women were widowed, and Miriam had invited the carpenter's wife and her son to live with her. Since the arrest at the Gethsemane garden the night before, neither woman had rested. They had endured the accusations, the hearings, the trials, the scourging, and now this crucifixion—all in less than a day's time.

Now with the arrival of this official from the temple, both Miriam and the younger Magdalene decided that enough was enough. As the centurion struggled to pull Magdalene back to keep her restrained, Miriam continued to beat Yoseph. Her hair, usually neatly coiled at the back of her neck, was now disheveled, spilling over her forehead and across her eyes.

As the attack continued, Miriam felt like she was in a surreal drama. She could hear the echo of her own cries and curses, as if she were standing outside herself.

"When I'm done with you," she screamed, "you'll feel like the Nazarene, only worse! Take that!" she bellowed, punching madly. "Can you feel the scorpions? Can you feel the cat-o'-nine-tails? Can you feel the pointed balls of lead?" She hit him again. "Answer me, you pompous pig!"

Yoseph lay there and took the blows. Although part of him wanted desperately to fight back, he didn't. For he realized that this was merely part of his punishment—the consequence of his own cowardliness.

FINALLY, THE centurion was able to pull Miriam away. The

guards now had their hands full as they restrained the two women, both still kicking wildly and hurling insults.

For a moment, Yoseph lay on the ground, breathless from the assault. Then he slowly rose to his knees.

"I don't know who you are," the centurion barked at Yoseph, "but you must leave at once!"

"I know who *he* is!" Miriam shouted. "He and all his pompous friends are the ones who crucified the Nazarene!"

She turned to Yoseph again. "He was innocent—you had no right to condemn Him!"

The centurion noticed that a boisterous crowd had started to gather again. Hearing the disturbance, some of the men and young boys who had left now returned to Golgotha in hopes of witnessing an encore to the bloodshed.

"Why are you here?" Magdalene challenged Yoseph. "Haven't you done enough already?"

"I am . . ." he stopped to catch his breath, "Yoseph of Arimathea."

"You're a coward!" yelled someone from the rabble.

"You're a murderer!" taunted another.

Motioning his guards to control the crowd, the centurion pulled the women aside and ordered them to be quiet or face expulsion from the site, never to see the corpse of the Nazarene again.

Turning back toward Yoseph, the centurion ordered him to leave immediately.

"But—" ·

"You must leave here now!" barked the centurion.

"But I can't—I have official business."

From his satchel, Yoseph pulled a rolled parchment, sealed with a waxy splotch embossed with the insignia of imperial Rome. It was from the office of Pilate the procurator. Waving for absolute silence from the crowd, the centurion tore the seal and began reading. By order of Pontius Pilate, custody of the body was to be transferred to Yoseph of Arimathea for secure burial.

"As you can see, I have permission to take the body," Yoseph explained.

"You can't!" cried Miriam.

"I mean no harm," Yoseph said. "If you would only give me a chance to explain, I can help you. Otherwise, the Romans will bury Him in a shallow grave next to the other criminals."

A look of horror passed over Miriam's face.

Yoseph continued quickly, "I have a family grave just north of the city. It's in a beautiful location—a garden."

But now Magdalene spat out, "The only thing that belongs in that grave tonight is your dead body!"

Miriam silenced Magdalene. During the months following her deliverance, Magdalene had looked to the much older Miriam for motherly counsel and guidance. Now was the time to yield to her wisdom once again. Magdalene could tell, from the look on her face, that Miriam's mental wheels were turning. Clear thinking and scheming were finally overriding her anger.

Perhaps this religious leader can help us, Miriam thought. Mary surely didn't have the money for a proper burial. Why not take from this devil all that we can get?

Miriam nodded slowly. "It is right that you pay for this."

In disbelief, Magdalene turned to Mary. Until now, the mother of Jesus had remained silent, quietly attended to by Maria, the mother of Joses. *Surely she would object to this preposterous idea*, thought Magdalene. *A caring mother wouldn't put her son's body into the hands of a stranger—let alone his murderers'—would she?*

But Mary's countenance was blank. She was tired and disheveled. Gazing at Miriam, she made no gesture of approval or disapproval. Any emotion was hidden beneath a layer of shock and grief.

Miriam locked eyes with Mary, silently reassuring her that this was a good plan. Trust me in this, her eyes seemed to say.

Wearily, Mary slowly nodded. Relying on the wisdom of her best friend, she relinquished her son.

INTENTLY, LONGINGLY, Mary now stared up at the bloodied corpse of her son suspended on the cross. In her mind, she was carried back to the night she first laid eyes on Him. Although it was three decades before, it seemed like it was just yesterday when she gave birth to Jesus. Ah, Bethlehem—a city in the hill country of Judah, also known as the "House of Bread."

That night, Mary and Joseph had had neither bread to eat nor a place to lodge. Had it not been for the hospitality of an old farmer, their son might have been born right there in the dusty streets.

"Push, Mary, push!" urged Joseph later as his wife struggled in labor.

She gasped—her breathing ragged.

"I . . . am . . . pushing!"

"Harder!" he said, gripping her hand more tightly.

She frowned up at him from her bed in the straw.

"Joseph, if you think you can do better," she snapped, "then next time we will beseech Yahweh God to allow you to experience childbirth!"

The Hebrews believed that special sufferings were the result of the primeval curse from the fall of Adam and Eve. For women, that suffering was the agony of giving birth. For men, it was the sweat of the brow. On the night Jesus was born, both Mary and Joseph bore their parts—Mary in the birth pangs and Joseph, as awkward as he was, in the labor of just trying to be a good husband.

As the baby's head appeared, Joseph felt a mixture of excitement and fear.

"Mary? What should I do?" He suddenly seemed much younger than his years.

Mary prayed, God, is this truly the man You chose to be the earthly father of Your son?

"Catch the baby in the blanket," she patiently instructed. "Don't let him touch the ground." She had learned much from overhearing tales from the Hebrew midwives.

One more push, and the baby was out. In that moment, Mary understood the words that her aunt had imparted to her just before they left Nazareth: With special suffering, there is also special blessing.

Carefully, Joseph cradled the tiny infant in his arms. Tears streamed down his cheeks.

"Mary," he whispered. "Look."

Grinning from ear to ear, the new father proudly lifted the baby up for his wife to see.

Suspended in the air before Mary, still connected by the cord of life and bloodied from birth, was the Savior of the world.

SNAPPING BACK to the present, aware of a growing anger within her, Mary stood and stared at the killer.

She started toward Yoseph.

The centurion rushed forward to intervene. He put his hand on her shoulder, but Mary slapped it away and glared at him. So much had been taken from her.

The centurion stepped back quickly. This was the mother of the crucified, after all. If anyone had a right to retaliate, she did.

Mary now stood so close to Yoseph that he could hear her quick breaths, see the fire in her eyes.

Yoseph, the once honorable counselor, dared not move a muscle.

Slowly, Mary raised her quivering hands to each side of

Yoseph's face. Her eyes were fixed and readied for an assault on this man who represented all that was hypocritical and repugnant to her.

Earlier in the day, the jagged pieces of bone from the cat-o'-nine-tails had gouged the flesh of her son, shredding Him beyond recognition.

Mary's thoughts jumbled together. He dare not flinch. This, he deserves!

Fearful of what was about to happen, Yoseph quickly glanced over at the centurion. But his attempt to stir the centurion's sympathies, his silent pleas for help against the embittered mother, were ignored.

There would be no mercy for the wretch. Yoseph was in this alone, and he knew it. In this fight, no one would defend him, nor should he expect that anyone would.

Magdalene, Miriam and Maria anxiously watched from the side. The honorable counselor would finally get his due.

CLOSING HIS eyes, Yoseph braced for the worst that one woman could do. His mind flooded with terrible recollections from the night before. At the inner court of the high priest, the Sanhedrin had met to devise their charges and begin their proceedings. Yoseph was present, as was most every other member of the Sanhedrin. He was the honorable counselor, the distinguished member in charge of the details and application of Mosaic law.

At every turn, however, the law was wrenched and contravened. First, it was declared illegal for the Jewish Council to meet and pass a capital sentence after sundown. So, to make everything "legal," they reconvened briefly at sunup the next morning.

Moreover, the witnesses they enlisted contradicted even themselves. They had little, if any, hard evidence against the accused man. According to Jewish law, testimony from false wit-

23

nesses was inadmissible. Today, however, the lies and fabrications went mostly unchallenged.

Finally, in a capital case, the accused could not be forced to testify. Even if he did speak, his testimony could not be used against him. Nevertheless, based on His own words, the Nazarene was convicted of blasphemy by the high priest.

In the midst of the proceedings, Yoseph had sat back quietly. He was aware of the corruption, yet he did little to stop it. Although he didn't consent to the plans of the Sanhedrin, neither did he raise serious objections. Laws were broken. Deals were struck. Justice was perverted. And the Jew was condemned.

By daybreak, it was all over. In the shadows of the night, out of the view of an already wary public, a dark conspiracy was birthed. Before this day, whenever the Sanhedrin convicted someone, Yoseph had believed he should be able to look at the accused without flinching, his conscience clear, knowing that the charges were just and the proceedings lawful. But this morning, Yoseph could not do that.

Standing now before the angry mother, Yoseph's eyes were again closed in fear and shame. Open them, he scolded himself. You must open them. Face her, you coward! What Yoseph didn't realize was that the woman herself was also struggling to open her eyes . . . the eyes of her soul.

EVER SINCE the angelic announcement three decades before, Mary had pondered and kept hidden so much in her heart—from the mystery of her son's conception, to His uncanny teachings, wise stories, and awesome miracles. But now, would she be required to keep this in her heart as well—her confusion, anger and grief? Impossible!

As tempting as it was to strike out against Yoseph, like her friends Magdalene and Miriam had just done, something about such outbursts seemed too easy and too insufficient to satiate her own anger. Certainly, Yoseph deserved his punishment. But what more could she add to it? Still, to do nothing seemed like it would only compound the injustices of the day, condemning her to a lifetime of resentment and suffering.

It was my son you killed, you murderous, self-absorbed—

Mary's thoughts faltered as she trembled and searched for just the right words to pierce Yoseph with. She found herself silently screaming, *He was my son!*

But something held her back.

Deep within her, memories of her son's teachings surfaced: "Ye have heard that it was said 'hate thine enemy.' But I say unto you . . ."

NO! She protested silently, suddenly feeling queasy. *Love? I cannot. I will not! Not this time!*

"Father, forgive them; for they know not what they do." The utterance from the cross was still fresh, just hours old. Her son had cried it out, even as the soldiers gambled for His clothing. The words of unusual grace now echoed against the curtain of the darkened sky, resonating within Mary and holding back the implacable spirit that threatened to descend upon her.

Yet still, her fingers pressed harder against Yoseph's face.

I have every right to hate you! she cried inside. *Every right!* Indeed, no one at Golgotha—not the centurion, the crowd, nor Yoseph himself—would have blamed Mary for anything she would have done right then. Some would have considered it not only her right, but also her duty to avenge the blood of her son; after all, she was His nearest relative.

Or am I? Something now was stirring within her.

Fifteen months previously, she and her other sons had arrived at a crowded synagogue where Jesus was teaching. Those outside sent word that the Nazarene's mother and brothers were seeking Him. However, Jesus disregarded the summons, instead saying only, "Who is my mother, or my brethren?"

When Mary and her sons finally pressed their way into the synagogue, someone pointed to them in response to Jesus' question. But Jesus paid no attention to them. Instead, He gestured toward those who sat around Him and said, "Behold my mother and my brethren!"

At first Mary was hurt and His brothers were angry. But Jesus winked at His mother and smiled at His brothers. Then turning back to His listeners, Jesus completed the teaching, "For whosoever shall do the will of God, the same is my brother, and my sister, and mother."

Now standing with her fingers pressed into the face of her son's killer, Mary realized the breadth of kindred ties. It was not just her son, but it was God's son, whom this manslayer had helped to convict and kill. She, in fact, was not the nearest relative. Yahweh God, His Father, was.

With this realization, the dark, toxic veil of resentment—everything Jesus sought to displace on the cross—began to lift. She no longer had to reclaim her son's blood. That was the Father's right and duty. Her soul was comforted and her mind empowered with the knowledge that human justice paled in comparison to God's justice. This coward, this pathetic twit of religious justice, would now find himself relinquished to the hands of One mightier and more fearsome than she.

PITIFULLY, RIGIDLY, Yoseph waited and braced for the worse. But the onslaught never came; the blows never materialized. Perhaps Mary's sorrow was too fresh and her energy too depleted to waste any more time on one so wretched as he.

Gradually Yoseph could feel the fingers against his face begin to relax. They still pressed against his cheeks tightly, but somehow seemed more embracing now. He thought she might have even been trembling.

Yoseph knew that he should open his eyes. Dignity demanded that he look at the mother and not shrink from her pain. Justice demanded that he look into the windows of her soul and no longer ignore the terror that he, in part, had helped birth.

Slowly, he opened his eyes. But instead of beholding the furrowed brow of this mother and her contempt, he beheld her own eyes—wet with tears—turned heavenward, as her mouth formed a silent prayer of supplication.

THREE

IN a quiet corridor in the back of the temple, still stunned with disbelief, Nicodemus reflected on the Golgotha travesty. He was a ruler of the Jews, a master teacher of Israel, a close associate to the high priest, and a Pharisee. Although wealthy and educated, he now felt impoverished in spirit and confounded in mind.

For three years, Nicodemus had secretly regarded the Nazarene. He was a timid, yet candid inquirer of Him. Reports of great miracles and wise teachings had abounded. But as the Nazarene's popularity soared, so did the jealousy and plotting of His adversaries.

Just one day earlier, some had argued that the Nazarene was a fraud. "The promised Messiah has to come from David's line in Bethlehem," they insisted, "not from Galilee!"

While Nicodemus didn't have a rebuttal to their arguments, he was fully convinced that their scheming and plotting was an abuse of due process. As a Pharisee, he was committed to keeping the law of God. However, in the case of the Nazarene, they were just as wrong in the spirit of their deliberations as they had been three years earlier when they first adjudicated a Sabbath case in Nazareth.

BOILING WATER on the Sabbath—was that such a crime? The young, frail child, barely six years old, from Sapphoris of Galilee, had been dehydrated from a fever and in need of extra fluids. Although the charge against the boy's father was just a minor one, the heavy-handedness of local synagogue leaders stirred up widespread public controversy. To retain order, the regional leaders from Nazareth had called upon Sanhedrin officials from Jerusalem to preside over the matter. Among them was Nicodemus.

Normally the synagogue was used for worship, but that day it was a court of law. By late afternoon, the hearing was over. The young father's defense was brushed aside. He was convicted and sentenced.

In his heart, Nicodemus felt badly for him. The infraction was petty. There was no premeditation or ill intent. Still, the law was the law, and the man was to be shunned.

After the proceedings were adjourned, the Sanhedrin officials were anxious to leave Nazareth, but the Sabbath was at hand. The thought of spending another night or two in this shabby little town displeased them.

Nazareth was a small village situated among the southern ridges of Lebanon, on a steep slope, about 14 miles from the Sea of Galilee and six miles west of Mount Tabor. Like all Galileans, its people were viewed as rude and less cultivated—lower in moral and religious character. Indeed, the Gentiles who mingled among them influenced many from this region.

During the synagogue hearings, there was very little room in Nazareth for Nicodemus and his associates to escape the icy glares of the locals. To stay an additional day, particularly after the controversial verdict had been handed down, would be insufferable. Nevertheless, the Sabbath enforcers couldn't just turn around and be Sabbath-breakers themselves—not here, at least. Attendance at Sabbath worship was mandated. They had no choice but to stay in Nazareth and remain as inconspicuous as possible.

Upon their return to the synagogue the next morning, the Sanhedrin officials were quickly escorted up front to the "chief seats" that were appropriated by the rulers. While shuffling through the assembly, Nicodemus ignored the stares by focusing on the structural dilapidation of the synagogue. The décor and arrangements of each synagogue depended on the wealth of its community. This synagogue was unimpressive, reflecting the poverty of Nazareth itself.

Seating was arranged so that everyone could see those in the chief seats and whoever was speaking. *This is one day I'd rather just sit in the back*, Nicodemus thought. Taking his seat up front, Nicodemus caught a dirty look from one of the locals who had attended the hearings. Here, just one day before, the angry public had assembled. In the center aisle a caring father was berated, and from these esteemed seats the contentious verdict was issued.

Now everyone's attention was front and center. *They're throwing daggers at us.* Nicodemus shivered. The synagogue seemed cold anyway, and the seats were hard. The only sense of warmth came from the local synagogue leaders themselves.

Worship commenced with the usual formalities. Throughout the morning, there were 18 prayers. From a wooden platform at the center of the synagogue, Scriptures were read and expositions were offered, one person at a time.

That momentous day, however, worship seemed endlessly dry. The week had been long for Nicodemus, and today's readings were uninspiring and the expositions hypnotically dull. With each reader, he suppressed his boredom and inwardly sighed. The disadvantage of sitting in the chief seats was that there was no opportunity for catching some sleep.

Act like you're interested, Nicodemus chided himself. He cracked his jaw, shifted his neck and forced an occasional nod of agreement.

Not until a certain Jew stood up to read did things become interesting. The attendant of the synagogue handed Him the scroll of Isaiah, and finding His place, the Nazarene began reading:

The Spirit of the Lord God is upon me; because the Lord hath anointed me to preach good tidings unto the meek; he hath sent me to bind up the brokenhearted, to proclaim liberty to the captives, and the opening of the prison to them that are bound; to proclaim the acceptable year of the Lord.

Stopping abruptly, the Nazarene gazed at the assembly, slowly closed the scroll, and went back and sat down—all without saying another word.

A cool breeze came through the window.

A few looked from side to side, waiting. Nervous glances filled the room—unsure what to do next.

Nicodemus massaged his beard, suddenly alert. *Now that's the way to do it,* he thought. *Just get to the point!*

What was unusual about this reading was its brevity. Those who stood at the front normally relished their time in the spotlight. They typically chose long passages from the Law and the prophets, extending their reading time to absurd lengths. However, no sooner had the Nazarene begun than He was finished. He did not belabor the reading.

Moreover, the Nazarene seemed unpretentious as He read. Unlike most of those who stood at the wooden podium, the Nazarene seemed genuinely humble—reading with authority, but also with sensitivity. Indeed, the passage He chose was timely, conveying the sort of mercy and grace that was so badly needed after such a difficult week of litigation.

Customarily after the Scriptures were read, the reader would then proceed with a lengthy exposition. However, the Nazarene did not do this. He just went back to His seat and sat down.

After a few hushed, uncertain moments, the synagogue began to buzz with whispering and murmuring: "The Nazarene has broken protocol! The Scriptures must be expounded upon. Someone must interpret them. Someone must explain them. They cannot stand alone, can they?"

The voices became louder. Arms waved and heads wagged. "Surely, this son of a carpenter has something to say, doesn't He?"

From his ringside seat, Nicodemus watched in amusement. Synagogue worship had become exciting. Anything out of the ordinary was truly welcome. Finally, a dull Sabbath was energized.

Most everyone assembled had come with a grievance because of the previous days' proceedings, and they were already primed for a fight. And what a fight they got!

With all the pressure that the local religious leaders had put on the Jerusalem officials during the week, they had this coming. Nothing was more entertaining and satisfying to Nicodemus than watching this spontaneous outburst of confusion happen on the watch of the local synagogue officials.

As the ruckus continued, Nicodemus spied out the nearest exit. *Just in case!* he chuckled to himself. A hasty retreat might be needed if the commotion got too out of hand.

Those nearest to the Nazarene motioned for Him to get back up, go forward and speak. But He didn't move.

Eventually an elderly temple attendant stood and motioned to the crowd. When everyone had quieted, the attendant picked up the scroll of Isaiah and beckoned for the next reader.

Then something unexpected happened.

"Today . . ."

A voice, clear and strong, called out from the back, where the Nazarene was seated. Once again, all eyes turned towards Him. The attendant up front was befuddled.

"Today," the Nazarene repeated, "this Scripture is fulfilled in your hearing."

The assembly once again erupted in pandemonium.

"Time to leave," Nicodemus chuckled to the leader seated next to him. The synagogue was in chaos as people questioned, loudly debated and even threatened to fight over the meaning of the Nazarene's words.

"Just what does He mean?" asked one.

"Who does He think He is?" cried another.

As the melee continued, Nicodemus and the other officials quietly ducked out of the synagogue to the safety of the streets.

As he walked alone toward his lodging, the words of Isaiah, as quoted by the Nazarene, echoed in his mind:

The Spirit of the Lord God is upon me . . .
the Lord hath anointed me . . .
he hath sent me . . .
to bind up the brokenhearted . . .
to proclaim liberty . . .

"Today this Scripture is fulfilled," was what the Nazarene had said. What part of Scripture had been fulfilled that day? Justice had been fulfilled, that was certain. The Sabbath law had also been fulfilled.

But that's all that was fulfilled, thought Nicodemus. *Indeed, the father of a sick boy—regardless of the pettiness of the charges, the mitigating circumstances or the public sentiment in his favor—had been successfully prosecuted. Yes, that too had been fulfilled!*

However, in the satisfaction of the law, at least to Nicodemus, something seemed terribly unfulfilled. Disappointment loomed in the wake of the whole ordeal. The words of Isaiah, as quoted by the Nazarene, seemed to magnify the emptiness of what should otherwise have been a celebration of justice.

We had done what we were supposed to, hadn't we?

The letter of the law was fulfilled, but the spirit of justice seemed strangely absent. Perhaps by His wise selection from the prophetic books, the Nazarene had reminded the assembly that the purpose of the law was to set people free, not to imprison.

But how can we let the convicted go free?

As perplexing as everything was, something else had made Nicodemus uneasy. The Nazarene's mannerisms, His humility, and His grace—none of these could be ignored.

Everything about Him is so different.

When He proclaimed, "This Scripture is fulfilled," He did so with a conviction and air of authority that suggested that He was speaking of Himself.

Of Himself? pondered Nicodemus. Such a notion was contrary to everything he had been taught. No one man could claim this of himself. Yet, perhaps that was the point. The Messiah was more than just a man. The mantle of heaven was to rest on Him who was the Anointed.

Of Himself!

The authority with which He spoke was not that of the ordinary civil or religious leaders, but of one representing a higher law and authority. It was an authority braided with compassion and grace. It was an application that was nonexistent in the law—the very law that Nicodemus and his associates were bound by oath to enforce. *I must meet this one who speaks "of Himself"!*

THE LATE evening private meeting he had had with the Nazarene was under cover of darkness because Nicodemus was a Pharisee, a teacher and ruler of the Jews. Meeting with the instigator might be construed as seditious and reported back to the high priest in Jerusalem. Tucked away in the cool shadows of a Nazareth alley, Nicodemus met face to face with Him. A few dogs barked in the distance, but they quieted immediately when the Nazarene gestured quickly at them.

Nicodemus was amazed. *How did He do that?* But the Nazarene just smiled.

For the next three hours, the two men spoke without interruption. The things the Nazarene said actually made sense. Nicodemus had taken pride in being well-respected and a descendant of Abraham, yet Jesus told him, "You must be born again." In other words, his descent from the line of Abraham wasn't enough to save him. Only those birthed from above would see the kingdom of God.

I believe I understand, Nicodemus affirmed in his heart. In the middle of the dark alley, Nicodemus felt as though his mind was basking in the light of a new day. *I do understand!*

Listening eagerly to the Nazarene, Nicodemus felt as though the steady eyes of this man could see into his heart. His words reached far beyond the level of mere doctrinal titillation. Instead, He conveyed a message that was life itself—deeply touching the core of the soul.

With their visit concluded, Nicodemus felt an inner awakening. Before this rendezvous, he had felt unclean from the weeklong court proceedings and their outcome.

But tonight, innocence was rebirthed.

His spirit was reborn!

OVER THE next three years, Nicodemus secretly kept apprised of the Teacher's activities. By the time this Passover week arrived, most everyone on the Sanhedrin was alarmed. Throngs of pilgrims who came up for the Feast turned out with palm branches in their hands to welcome the Teacher and His entourage into Jerusalem.

Some hailed Him as a king. Others called Him a prophet.

Still others proclaimed, "He is the Messiah, the Anointed One."

With so many people making their annual pilgrimage, such a clamor was embarrassing for the religious elite. People were asking them hard questions about the promised Messiah: What do the prophets say? What should we expect? Hasn't it been long enough? Why not this Nazarene? Just listen to His wisdom. How can you ignore the miracles?

Had it been at any other time, the uprising could have been ignored. For years the religious elite had shrugged off the reports about the Nazarene. He had, up until this week, been merely an annoyance. But now the crowds were turning in His favor.

"Just look at what He did yesterday in the temple," the moneychangers complained about his overturning their tables and vilifying their profession. "You must do something!" Within days, the murmuring among the Sanhedrin officials quickly escalated into a full-blown conspiracy. In spite of the caution urged by the moderate Pharisees seated on the Council, a few outspoken members were bent on pushing their murderous plot through.

Until that day, Nicodemus had kept quiet. But indifference was no longer an option. He had to do something.

"Are you sure He's a fraud?" ventured Nicodemus.

A contentious member shot back, "Are you from Galilee, too? Look into it, and you will find that a prophet does not come out of Galilee."

"But does our law condemn anyone without first hearing him?" Nicodemus replied.

That was weak, Nicodemus rebuked himself. *I must do better. Defend Him!*

AS THE Jerusalem sky darkened, Nicodemus continued be-rating himself for the travesty of justice he had taken part in.

He wished there was something he could do, but now it was too late. The Nazarene was already crucified.

While still brooding in the temple, Nicodemus caught a whiff of the rich, meaty smell of the last sacrifices being burned, as well as the sweet fragrance of incense being offered up. The Passover festivities were concluding. Most of the ones who had come to present their offerings or make peace with their God had left.

The pilgrims who lingered behind, indulging in last-minute sightseeing before returning to their homes, noticed that the sky had grown increasingly darker. Although there had been a moderate cloud cover above, the sun was now strangely eclipsed.

Suddenly the temple floor jerked violently.

Screams erupted. Next to Nicodemus, an elderly man fell backwards. People shouted. Babies cried. Nicodemus himself crouched low on the shaking floor. Throughout the temple, others tripped and stumbled as the stone pavement slipped and shifted repeatedly beneath them.

In the outer court, the moneychangers' tables rattled noisily. Earthenware toppled and fell to the ground, broken.

Inside the temple, Nicodemus struggled to stand. His stomach felt queasy and his legs were like rubber, unable to support him. On all fours, he crawled to the nearest arched corridor. Loose rubble from the walls spilled down around him. Above him, the huge stone slab that formed the low arch was cracking.

Half running now, he scrambled out into the open court-yard where other worshippers huddled for safety. Behind him, the arch tottered and collapsed, shattering and spraying its debris.

Safely out of harm's way, Nicodemus squatted on his heels and watched the priests who had been working in the court-yard. Those who served near the altar of burnt offerings flung their utensils aside and staggered away. Fire spilled over the edge of the altar. A dead ox, which was not yet tied down to the grate of the altar, slithered sideways and tumbled onto the temple floor. Nicodemus shook his head at the chaos of the scene. *And this is the religious system that's supposed to save us all?*

Other priests struggled for their footing as well, tangled up in their long robes. Normally emboldened by their pomp and piety, they were now just as faltering and weak-kneed as everyone else. As awful as the earthquake was, Nicodemus found himself amused by their trepidation, which stood in stark contrast to the fortitude of the Nazarene. Only a few hours earlier, the Jesus had resolutely set out for Golgotha with His cross on His shoulders.

As the dust settled in the courtyard, Nicodemus continued to ponder the ironies of the scene before him. The Passover lambs, once considered perfect, were now just as broken as those whose sin they would bear. There must be something more.

Reaching back, the words that the Nazarene spoke of Himself echoed again in Nicodemus' mind, "The Spirit of the Lord God is upon me . . ."

Without a doubt, the Galilean, the one they called Jesus of Nazareth, was the true Lamb of God! All the blood splattered on the sacrificial altars throughout the centuries could never accomplish as much as His one sacrifice at Golgotha. All the incense ever burned and spices ever offered could never truly satisfy the monumental debt of sin man owed or bring lasting peace with God.

I understand now!

Nicodemus stood up and quickly dusted his robes off. After checking on the others who were still recovering on the ground beside him, he dashed off to the temple storage area.

Until this moment, Nicodemus had felt helpless in

knowing what to do in the wake of the crucifixion. At last, he had an idea. He couldn't reverse the crucifixion, but now there was something he could do.

At the temple storage area, he purchased myrrh and other ointments that would be suitable for embalming. Perfumes and ointments were often used in the temple work for offerings and prayers. Today they would be used to anoint the corpse. Their sweet aromas would ascend to the heavens, perhaps soothing the anger of Almighty God and making amends for himself; at least Nicodemus hoped so.

Just then, a cry sounded in the temple. There was trouble. Nicodemus sprinted from the storage area to the inner court. The high priest looked agitated and crazed. Wildly, he waved his hands as he tried to explain to the other priests what had just happened. Rocking, bending and bowing in anguish, he alternated between reaching toward the sky and flailing his forehead. Closer now, Nicodemus discerned that the crisis was related to the oracle, the most holy place in the temple.

As he followed the priests and some of the Pharisees to the innermost area, Nicodemus finally saw what had caused the high priest such anxiety. To their horror, the huge curtain—the holy veil of blue, purple and scarlet—separating the sacred chamber from the rest of the sanctuary was torn in two, from top to bottom. What was once hidden from public view and only accessible to the most privileged was now exposed for all to behold. The Ark of the Covenant, the sacred, gold-lined chest holding the tablets of testimony, the very symbol of God's presence, was now visible.

Standing transfixed, mouth opened, Nicodemus gaped in astonishment. Never before had he seen such a beautiful sight—the golden seat of pure mercy, stained with blood. Absolutely magnificent!

Around him, the priests scurried to find something, anything, to cover and conceal the Ark from view. First one, and then another, stripped themselves of their holy robes and tunics, forming a makeshift wall to once again block everyone's view of the "beauty of Israel."

Chuckling at the absurdity of it all, Nicodemus walked away. *They just don't understand,* he laughed.

The Lamb of God had been slain. Atonement forever was made. Like wrapping paper torn from a long-awaited gift, the veil of blue, purple and scarlet was now ripped wide open. Mercy was now in plain sight for all to behold. Pity those who were so busy protecting God's mercy that they couldn't stop to partake of it.

ON HIS way out of the city, nearing the place of execution, Nicodemus crossed paths with first one, and then another, group of soldiers carrying away the grisly remains of the crucified. When he arrived at the place of the skull, only one prisoner remained nailed on a cross—the one in the middle, the Nazarene.

Nicodemus winced at the sight. The corpse was bloodied and hung limply. Crucifixion was a brutal and torturous execution. No wonder the law said, "He who is hanged is accursed of God."

As Nicodemus scanned the hill, he saw the Nazarene's mother sitting off to one side of the cross, still in shock and inconsolable. Surrounding her were some of the women, and someone else.

A Roman soldier?

This was not just any soldier. It was a centurion. And he was handing something to Mary.

A flower? He's giving her flowers?

It was a lily blossom—white with streaks of pink.

Nicodemus was aghast. *What nerve!*

For Nicodemus the madness of the day had no boundaries. *A soldier kills a woman's son and then gives her flowers?*

Suddenly, his blood was boiling. The euphoria he had felt earlier as he beheld the mercy seat was crumbling under the weight of his anger. A ladder was leaning against the cross to remove the frail body. A guard climbed up with a long piece of linen and wrapped it around the chest and under the arms of the bloody corpse. This would support the body once the nails were removed.

With the torso secure, the guard moved his ladder to the side and began extracting the first nail. It was lodged tightly against the wrist of the corpse, partially dimpled into the outer layers of skin, compressing the tendons beneath. From behind the beam, the guard first pounded up and under the bent nail to straighten it. He then hammered against the end of the nail to pound it back through the beam. On the other side, the head of the nail now protruded out from the wrist.

Reaching over the horizontal beam and the arm of the corpse, the guard began prying out the nail. Even from where Nicodemus stood, he could hear the suction noise as the nail was forcibly yanked from the wrist, allowing the first arm to dangle freely. Nicodemus squirmed.

As the guard moved his ladder and began freeing the other arm, Nicodemus wondered what they would do with the body. In all likelihood, they would dispose of the corpse in a way that was customary for every other person who was executed for a capital offense. The burial of criminals was void of dignity. Usually their bodies were put in a grave just shallow enough for savage beasts to smell them out, dig them up and devour their flesh. From the brutal haste with which the Nazarene's corpse was being removed from the cross, it appeared that His burial would be just as ignominious.

Do something, Nicodemus said to himself. *Don't just stand there.*

This Nazarene was the Lamb of God. Even the slain carcasses of the temple lambs were treated with more dignity than He would get.

Nicodemus was further agitated when he noticed what appeared to be a religious leader standing at the base of the cross. Overseeing the removal of the corpse was a member of the Sanhedrin. Whoever it was, his robes were disheveled and he was wiping his eyes and face.

Tears? How dare he cry!

The religious leaders didn't care for the Nazarene or His family. Of that, Nicodemus was certain.

He's dead already! Nicodemus screamed inside. *Leave Him alone. What right do you have to even be here?*

The religious leader was holding some sort of document—probably orders from the high priest to supervise the quick disposal of the body. Whoever this was, he was obviously up to no good.

Staring at the travesty before him, Nicodemus felt his face tighten and his skin flush. Rage surged through his body. Yesterday he had been too slow to object, too afraid to speak out on behalf of the Nazarene.

Today would be different. Today, Nicodemus would step in and stop the madness.

Yesterday, the religious leaders had outnumbered Nicodemus, but today this official stood alone. The playing field was finally level. The elitist was an easy target.

Mustering his courage, Nicodemus stormed toward the base of the cross and grabbed the man. He threw him to the ground.

"You cursed wretch!" cried Nicodemus.

Gasping for air, the man on the ground lay stunned.

Nicodemus cocked his foot and prepared to deliver a few well-placed kicks to the man's side.

But suddenly, Nicodemus himself was slammed to the

ground. He grimaced as the centurion subdued him, pinning him facedown on the gravel.

"You have no business here!" the centurion yelled at Nicodemus.

Nicodemus struggled and yelled back, "None of you have any business here either! This man was innocent. You've crucified an innocent man."

The centurion, his knee still pressed against Nicodemus' neck, replied, "Not only was He an innocent man, He was a righteous man, too."

"I don't care what you think, you pagan—"

Mid-sentence, Nicodemus stopped fighting, dumb-struck. He twisted his head up and stared at the centurion.

What did he just say?

As if the centurion could read his mind, he pulled Nicodemus to his feet and said, "You have no quarrel with me. Indeed, this was an innocent man." Then with eyes tearing, gazing up at the cross, the centurion added, "Truly, He was the Son of God!"

Nicodemus swiveled his head back and forth, staring at both the religious leader and the centurion in disbelief. He wasn't sure who to be angry with anymore—or even if he had a right to feel any rage.

Shifting his attention back to the religious leader, Nicodemus shuddered suddenly. He finally realized whom he had just attacked.

"Counselor?"

"Nicodemus?" Yoseph stared back, equally surprised by the identity of his aggressor.

"Why are you here, Yoseph? You are the chief counselor for the Sanhedrin," Nicodemus frowned at him. "You should be ashamed of yourself—you and all the rest for what you've done!"

"I have orders, Nicodemus—" Yoseph sputtered.

Nicodemus jabbed his finger at the man. "You will not desecrate the body of the Nazarene!"

"Nicodemus, you don't understand. I have the consent of Pilate to—"

"No! You don't understand!" Nicodemus interrupted. Sinking to his knees, Nicodemus cried out, "This was not just any man. This was the Lamb of God. This was the Son of God. We crucified an innocent man!"

"I understand, Nicodemus," Yoseph tried, "but I must—"

"You were wrong!" blasted Nicodemus, now weeping. He hit the dirt with his fists.

Yoseph stood speechless, staring at him.

"We were all wrong!" yelled Nicodemus. "DEAD WRONG!"

FOUR

FOR 22 years, Yoseph and Nicodemus had worked together on the Sanhedrin. Yet, until now, neither man had disclosed to the other his private thoughts, including his feelings about the Nazarene. But now, at the base of the cross, both men freely discussed their meetings with Him and confessed how intrigued they had become with His life and teachings.

"It's all right, Nicodemus. I don't blame you. You had every reason to be angry with me. No one was more wrong than I," said Yoseph. "I was a coward. I should have stood up to the Council, but my silence condemned Him."

"In a thousand years, I would have never believed you felt about Him the way I did," said Nicodemus. "I thought I was the only one so enamored with His teachings."

Yoseph shook his head and sighed. "I bet there are others."

Nicodemus was puzzled. "On the Sanhedrin?"

"Of course."

"How many, do you suppose?"

"Who knows? But I'm convinced that you and I weren't the only ones with these views."

As a 29-year veteran on the Sanhedrin, Nicodemus was one of the most esteemed teachers of the law. Yoseph joined the Sanhedrin seven years after Nicodemus and became known as the "Honorable Counselor," specializing in the intricacies and applications of Mosaic law.

The Sanhedrin was the supreme judicial and administrative Council of the Jews. Its 71 members consisted of chief priests, scribes, elders, and a high priest who was its president. It was the high court of the land. Its civil and ecclesiastical decrees were binding over all the Jews, whether they lived in Palestine or were scattered abroad. It was the company of Israel's most elite.

The coveted Council seats, however, were lonesome ones. Behind closed doors, if its members could be perfectly honest, none of the power or prestige made any of them feel truly satisfied. There was an incompleteness in most everything they did. Surrounded by 69 other members, Nicodemus and Yoseph both felt the pompous hierarchy was detached from reality and superficial in its relationships.

As professional representatives of the Mosaic law, each member experienced the universal pressure to conform to certain ideologies and standards. The chief priests were hawkish in their policies. Any deviation from tradition was frowned upon. Dissenting views were unwelcome.

On a social level, friendships among the Sanhedrin's members were shallow at best. Competing agendas, conceited attitudes and fierce jealousies were barriers to any advancement of brotherhood.

Nicodemus had become increasingly disenchanted with this fragmented association of Yahweh's representatives. Each Sanhedrin member was a real person with real thoughts and feelings, but no one was allowed to bleed if they were cut emotionally. Personal weakness, if there was any, was kept out of view. To speak honestly about one's particular needs was unacceptable. To be transparent about one's private temptations or failings was unheard of.

Now, finally, after two decades of pretentious living, at least two Sanhedrin members were shedding their masks and talking openly about their convictions, without fear of reprisal. How many others were also secret followers? Nicodemus and Yoseph could only speculate.

Was the crucifixion really just railroaded by a stubborn minority of the Sanhedrin? If others had mustered their courage and broken their silence, could the execution have been stayed? As the last nail was extracted and the corpse lowered to the ground, the two men pondered the possibilities.

"I don't know," said Nicodemus. "Even if enough others had spoken up, I'm still not convinced anything would have changed."

"What are you suggesting?" Yoseph frowned. "Are you now trying to excuse our weakness?"

Nicodemus raised both hands in defense, about to explain himself.

"We were wrong," continued Yoseph. "We must agree on that!"

Nodding, Nicodemus said, "Of course, we were cowards. But doesn't it seem as if there's something almost providential about the Nazarene's death? Like there's a larger plan that's now been set in motion?"

Yoseph squinted at him in confusion. "I don't understand."

Nicodemus then told Yoseph of the bizarre events that had happened—the violent earthquake that shook Jerusalem, the temple veil that tore from top to bottom, and the mercy seat that became exposed for all to see.

"Doesn't the occurrence of these things, simultaneous with the Nazarene's death, seem just a bit too coincidental?" he asked.

Yoseph rubbed his chin, silently absorbing the other man's words.

Nicodemus continued, "The events of the day somehow seem fraught with meaning. While it's true that we were responsible for convicting and killing the Nazarene, somehow, our human failure just seems to have framed everything that has happened. It's as if—"

Yoseph picked up the thought. "—as if a divine hand was behind it all?"

Nicodemus nodded, pleased that he finally understood.

As the men contemplated these mysteries, the corpse was lowered into the arms of the centurion, who then carried it to where Mary and the women huddled. Yoseph and Nicodemus started to walk over to the women to offer their consolations and prayers, but Miriam quickly stood and stopped them.

Miriam had been a wealthy supporter of the Nazarene. Since His arrest the night before, she had assumed the roll of protector to the Nazarene's mother. Today her guard was up. Her outstretched hand, palm raised, and bitter glares sent the unmistakable signal to both men to back off.

Nicodemus and Yoseph knew their presence was awkward. They were intruders—conspirators and murderers by association. There was very little that either could say or do that would offer comfort to an angry, grieving mother.

Nevertheless, Miriam also now sensed that the two men were of a different spirit than most of the other Sanhedrin members. While she didn't shoo them away entirely, neither did she allow them close enough to risk further harm. *Far too early to be on friendly terms,* thought Miriam, as she held them at bay. Everyone's nerves were still just a bit too raw.

To the surprise of Nicodemus and Yoseph, however, Miriam did allow the centurion to approach Mary with the lily blossom. He wasn't an instigator of the crucifixion; rather, he was just following orders. In truth, the centurion had even gone the extra mile to ensure that some of the customary brutalities associated with crucifixion didn't happen.

Eventually the corpse of the Nazarene was loaded onto a bier. Under the supervision of the centurion, the soldiers hoisted it onto their shoulders and carried it northward from

Golgotha. The women lead the procession. Nicodemus and Yoseph followed behind.

"Any idea where they will take him?" asked Nicodemus.

"That's what these papers are concerning," replied Yoseph. "I had just come from Pilate's house a short time before you grabbed me."

"Why were you there?" asked Nicodemus

"I went to get permission to give the Nazarene a decent burial."

"You went to Pilate for the corpse?" Nicodemus was shocked. That was quite a brave act.

Yoseph nodded in response.

As dangerous as the request was, Yoseph had resolved that he was tired of being a coward. This was his chance for redemption—to perform at least one act of civility for the Nazarene. Failure in this would just lead to more regret. Giving Him a decent burial wouldn't reverse the crucifixion, but it would at least bring a measure of decency to a day that was otherwise devastating.

"Weren't you afraid?"

"Of course I was. But I was more worried about what would happen to the body of the Nazarene," admitted Yoseph. "You know how sometimes a corpse will be left hanging for days while bugs and birds eat away at it. I just couldn't let that happen."

"How did you get permission?"

"It wasn't easy," explained Yoseph. "Just getting an audience with Pilate was difficult, as you can well imagine."

The procurator didn't want to spend any additional time on anything related to the Nazarene, particularly since he'd already been up most of the previous night haggling with the priests and Herod. He was drained. If this wasn't enough, he then had to deal with the unexpected earth tremors—assessing

49

the damage and overseeing the repairs. All of this happened during the busiest week of the year, too.

Yoseph laughed. "My timing was horrible. I came knocking just after he had returned home and settled down for supper."

"So how did you get a meeting with him?" asked Nicodemus.

"His attendant told me that official public hours were over and that I'd have to wait until after the Sabbath."

"Yes, of course. But how did you get in?"

"I slipped the attendant three shekels," Yoseph paused, grinning, "and suggested he reconsider the hour."

"And . . ." Nicodemus prodded.

"When he returned from telling Pilate that someone else wanted to meet with him, he again insisted that the procurator was too busy dealing with the earthquake situation."

"What did you do?"

"I slipped him another three shekels and suggested that Pilate would be grateful to the servant who reminded him that I was a man of wealth and influence, and that it would not be politically expedient for him to infuriate one of his allies in the Sanhedrin."

Nicodemus shook his head, disappointed. "So, once again, you've relied on your money and power to open doors for you?"

Yoseph frowned. "I tell you this, Nicodemus — all the wealth that I've accumulated means nothing to me now, when I consider what a coward I've been."

Nicodemus was being unfair, and he knew it. But before he could clarify what he meant, Yoseph angrily continued, "I have nothing to be proud of—nothing!" He jabbed his finger at the other man.

"And neither do you, Nicodemus! Let's keep that straight."

"Calm down, Yoseph!" said Nicodemus. Each man was fighting his own demons that day, he realized.

A few minutes of tense silence ensued. And then Nicodemus spoke up again, eager to hear the rest of the story.

"So," he ventured, "just how did you finally get an audience with Pilate?"

"The attendant said that Pilate had planned to follow customary protocol and bury the body next to other reprobates."

"So, He'd be thrown into a common grave," Nicodemus said.

Yoseph nodded, then continued. "I told him that if he wasn't careful, such an indignity might further incite the Nazarene's followers. Any disturbance that resulted would surely be reported back to Rome. I argued that Pilate might get what he wants, but he might not want what he gets. If he truly wanted matters to stay civil, he should transfer custody of the corpse to me so that I could bury it in a suitable grave."

"And your argument obviously worked. . ."

"The next thing I knew, the attendant emerged with parchment in hand!" said Yoseph proudly, unrolling it for Nicodemus to see.

NORTHWARD, PAST the Fish Gate, the procession marched slowly.

"So where are we taking Him?" asked Nicodemus.

"To a garden on the edge of Jerusalem," replied Yoseph, "just outside the north wall. I own it. Inside the garden, there's a sepulcher, newly carved out of a cave. It has six ledges inside."

"You're giving the Nazarene your own sepulcher?" Nicodemus was surprised.

"Yes. Mary doesn't have the money to give Him a proper burial," explained Yoseph. "So I am giving her one of the ledges in the burial chamber for her son. It will be private, secluded and secure."

As they journeyed on, Nicodemus marveled at how little he really knew about Yoseph and at how he had underestimated and misjudged him.

Yoseph was indeed a man of wealth. He was from Arimathea, a fair-sized city just 20 miles from Jerusalem in the hill country of Ephraim. The lucrative business of perfumery had been passed down from generation to generation in his family. Such perfumes were used for personal enjoyment as well as religious worship. Being the most prominent supplier of perfumes and ointments in Jerusalem, Yoseph was well-known to Pilate and thus had some influence with him.

During his tenure on the Sanhedrin, Yoseph became the exclusive supplier of perfumes used in the temple. This monopoly caused Nicodemus and others to be wary of Yoseph. Being the sole provider of the temple perfumes seemed to be a conflict of interest.

Yet, what member of the Sanhedrin didn't occasionally exploit his position for personal gain? Different ones had trades and crafts. They, too, trafficked their goods. Others had egos that needed to be stroked and enjoyed feeling important. In one form or another, each member personally benefited from his position. With that in mind, Nicodemus had buried his suspicions long ago.

Today, however, his questions resurfaced. *Just what is he up to?* Nicodemus wondered.

Yoseph might be trying to profit from the prestige associated with the donated burial cave. He was a man of wealth, so the donation of the cave was not a financial burden for him. But by supplying the tomb, Yoseph could have easily positioned himself for personal gain. Surely, someone would eventually ask about the generous benefactor. Was this a power move by Yoseph? A stroke to his ego?

In addition, he was also profiting from the sale of the burial spices. Nicodemus had personally sacrificed to purchase these spices from the temple treasury. But because Yoseph was the sole provider of the spices, he would indirectly benefit from Nicodemus' purchase as well.

But Nicodemus knew he must set aside his growing suspicions, at least for now. This was no time for petty jealousy. Now was the time to unite and work together, especially when all the other disciples were in such disarray.

Steering his mind in a more positive direction, Nicodemus asked Yoseph, "Just how did you come to first meet the Nazarene?"

"I first heard of Him when you did," said Yoseph.

Nicodemus searched his memory. "There in Nazareth—after the trial? At the synagogue?"

"That's the place!"

"We were there together, weren't we?" said Nicodemus. "Remember how dull everything was just before the Nazarene spoke?"

"I dozed off," confessed Yoseph. "Only after the clamor erupted did I awaken. I never did understand what all the commotion was about. Just when everything settled down, the Nazarene spoke out again—declaring that something had been fulfilled. The next thing I knew, you were dragging me out the side door."

Nicodemus explained to Yoseph about the disturbance that day. At last, Yoseph understood what had happened in the synagogue. After the incident, no one—neither Nicodemus nor anyone else—had been willing to talk about it.

Nicodemus then confessed to Yoseph about his late night meeting with the Nazarene. He beamed as he recalled Jesus' words and the change that had begun in his heart.

Nicodemus then asked, "Tell me—what got your attention? When did you become a secret follower?"

"It was the next day," Yoseph said. "If I recall, didn't you leave town first thing after the Sabbath?"

"That's correct. I would have left a day earlier if I could have."

Yoseph nodded. "I stayed behind. Instead of traveling back to Jerusalem as the rest of you did, I decided to visit my family in Arimathea. They lived close by, as you know."

He paused and then pointed out to Nicodemus the garden cemetery in the distance, still about one and one-half furlongs away.

"While preparing to leave Nazareth," continued Yoseph, "I heard about the funeral for the boy who had died, whose father we had charged and convicted for boiling the water."

Nicodemus shook his head. "Next to what we did today, that was the most despicable thing we've ever done."

"Agreed!" said Yoseph. "In fact, when I learned that the boy had died, I felt so guilty about it, I secretly provided the burial spices and paid for the funeral. What I did for the little boy and his father is what I'm doing for Mary and her son now. I had to make things right, but it had to be done secretly. I didn't tell you or anyone else because I didn't know whom I could trust."

"Then the boy had a decent funeral?" asked Nicodemus.

"No, I wouldn't quite say that."

Nicodemus was visibly confused.

Smiling, Yoseph said, "In truth, you might say that he had a great funeral!"

Nicodemus stared at him in horror. "A 'great' funeral? How can a funeral ever be called 'great'?"

"Ah! Everything about this one was great!" laughed Yoseph. "You see, I was following the funeral procession a short distance away when the Nazarene approached and stopped the procession."

"What did He say?"

"I was too far away to hear what was said. All I know is what I saw."

"Yes?" Nicodemus' revulsion had given way to curiosity.

"They first lowered the stretcher to the ground with the corpse on it. Then the Nazarene dropped to one knee, smiled, and stretched His hand toward the dead boy."

"And . . .?"

"And the boy reached back!"

"He what?" Nicodemus stared at him in disbelief.

"It happened, I tell you—the boy reached back! He was alive!"

"And you witnessed this?"

Yoseph laughed, "Of course!"

"And then what did the boy do?"

"He sat up!"

"And the Nazarene?"

"He picked him up and held him high for everyone to see—alive!"

Yoseph then told Nicodemus how, from that day forward, his interests in the cold formalities and superficialities of the Sanhedrin had begun to wane.

"It's a supreme irony, isn't it?" said Nicodemus. "We, who were so obsessed with the trivialities of the Sabbath code, shrugged off a man who was fighting for the life of his son. On the contrary, the Nazarene, who—"

Yoseph picked up the thought. "—who was indifferent to the tenets of ceremonial defilement, embraced the man and revived his son, restoring him to his family and friends."

Nicodemus smiled warmly.

"Ah. . . it was a great funeral indeed!" beamed Yoseph. "Ever since that day, I've felt more alive than ever!"

FIVE

THAT'S THE last of the heart cake," Ammi said, as he followed Marcus out the door. "If you want more, come back after the Sabbath."

The Jerusalem district of Mishneh had two bakers, and Ammi's Kneading Trough was the most convenient one for Marcus on his way home from the garden tomb. Heart cake was not actually cake, but loaf bread made from the finest wheat. It was his mother's favorite.

Although Marcus' family didn't live in this district, he was familiar with this area, as he was with most other parts of Jerusalem. Over the years, the townspeople watched as the dark, curly-haired little boy grew up into the young man that he was today. Just eight years earlier, when he first became a teenager, Marcus was unusually tall and lanky for his age. He would laugh as he stood toe-to-toe with his mother Miriam, periodically checking his height, amused that he was beginning to see over her forehead.

In his late adolescence, Marcus became increasingly aware that the younger girls were beginning to look at him differently as well—not just as the bratty little son of a wealthy plantation owner, but as an emerging young man to whom they might someday be betrothed. His growth spurt ushered in all the hormones, tensions and curiosities of boyhood adolescence. Now as a young man, Marcus struggled to steady those urges as he watched the young girls of his childhood blossom into the attractive ones of his manhood.

At first he enjoyed growing up and the possibilities and privileges that it afforded. But then he felt trapped by the pressure to act responsible, particularly after his father's death a few years earlier, when the need arose for him to assume the role of "man of the house."

In truth, in the same way that her son had once been unusually tall for that early stage of his adolescence, Miriam sensed that he was now unusually immature for this early stage of his manhood. Standing only chest-high to her grown-up son, she could no longer look straight into his eyes—but she could still look straight into his heart. And there, she beheld a fatuous and foolish side of her son that she feared might someday get him into trouble.

From the crucifixion site, Miriam bid her son to run and purchase some last-minute supplies before the Sabbath began. He would have arrived earlier had the ruckus at Golgotha not broken out. Marcus stayed behind and hid amongst the boisterous crowd to watch the religious leader get ambushed. He was astounded by his mother's spirit and proud of her defiant stand.

Nevertheless, his amusement cost him precious time. The day of Preparation was almost over. Merchants were already closing their shops as Sabbath lamps were being lit.

While waiting for the baker to wrap the cakes, Marcus noted how still and quiet the streets seemed compared to the chaos of the Passover festivities earlier that week. The narrow streets and dark arched bazaars that had welcomed throngs of families from various nations were now virtually empty.

All week long the temple itself had been a noisy market. The outer court became a barnyard filled with pens and stalls for sheep, goats, and cattle that would be used for offerings.

"Who needs a fine young ox?" bellowed one husbandman. "The firstling of the flock!"

Another rancher crowed, "Unblemished sheep. Three for the price of two. Ready for sacrifice!"

Everywhere, farmers shouted the merits of their beasts. Sheep bleated. Oxen lowed. Sellers of doves competed to offer the newest deals and deepest discounts. Potters offered bountiful choices and endless supplies of clay dishes and ovens for roasting and eating the Passover lamb. Venders of wine, oil, salt, and everything needed for sacrificing beckoned their customers. Booths to exchange foreign money for acceptable temple currency were everywhere.

The chaos only mounted when the Teacher from Nazareth arrived with His entourage. Although He tried to be unassuming, the crowds pressed in around Him as though He was a celebrity. For some, their hearts' door swung wide open to new and deeper understanding. For others, that door slammed shut, forever bolted tight against the Teacher. Within just days, His presence had left the temple priests and Pharisees bitterly disturbed. They feared that the disorder would be reported back to Rome.

If the confusion of Passover wasn't enough, the midday earth tremors that rattled the city and neighboring villages left many houses and structures moderately damaged. In the midst of the turmoil, many pilgrims left Jerusalem earlier than they had planned.

Tonight, however, the streets were quieter. Passover had concluded and the Paschal lambs were slain. Unleavened bread had been consumed and blood was splattered on doorposts throughout the city. With the Nazarene finally executed and His followers disbanded, the city was back to normal. Families and homes were once again beginning their customary Sabbath festivities.

After paying 19 copper coins, Marcus hurried down the

cobblestone street toward the Upper City. Catching a whiff of the freshly baked unleavened cake, he called back to the baker, "Peace." Ammi's Kneading Trough still made bread the old way—baked in the fire-heated ground, covered with embers. It was the best in Jerusalem.

"God be gracious to you," the baker echoed back to Marcus, now nearly out of sight.

Hurrying through the streets, Marcus saw tired laborers walking briskly to reach their homes before the Sabbath commenced. On the Sabbath, needless and avoidable work was forbidden. The Mosaic law laid down strict regulations regarding its observance. In the synagogues, prophets and teachers would read and expound on God's law and Sabbath restrictions.

"Remember the Sabbath day," Marcus' parents had nagged, "and keep it holy!" Weekly, he was warned that rabbinical minders watched for Sabbath infractions. Traveling was forbidden. Work was forbidden. *Is there anything that isn't forbidden?* wondered Marcus.

What was supposed to be a day of rest had, in his mind, become a day of work—as the average person labored under the anxieties and obsessions associated with keeping this day holy. The endless restrictions enforced by the Pharisees made it anything but a blessed day.

"God be gracious" . . . *to me?* Marcus mulled over the baker's salutation in his mind.

While Ammi meant well, this parting wave was especially annoying. God is *anything* but gracious! The only thing gracious about this night, thought Marcus, is that the Nazarene is dead!

For years, his mother had strongly adhered to the Jewish traditions. She and her husband had wealth and owned eight olive groves in the Judean region. They were faithful in their tithing, devoting their first-fruits to the temple.

When her husband died, Miriam sank into moderate depression. She was now a single mother and overseeing her late husband's groves. She felt overwhelmed by the increased responsibilities and having less time to do them in. Over time, she grew indifferent to those Jewish restrictions that she found to be so wearisome.

The upheaval and loneliness eventually drove Miriam to search for a more meaningful connection with Yahweh God, beyond the routine traditions of her culture. The prophets had written that Yahweh God would be as a husband to the widows and a father to the orphans. But just making the occasional offering of a pigeon or the first-fruits no longer brought her the satisfaction she inwardly craved.

Traveling in Galilee two and one-half years earlier, she first met the Teacher. She witnessed His miracles on different occasions; but she was primarily enamored with His teachings and mannerisms. Although He was devout, He was different from the other teachers of the law. He seemed to truly care about people. He reached out to those like herself who felt displaced by the Jewish traditions. Miriam quickly became one of His first converts. Her once fading spiritual embers now blazed anew with life.

As Marcus watched these changes in his mother, he was not impressed at all. Since his father's death, he assumed that his mother's grief was a signal of her never-ending attachment to her late husband's memory. The further she sank in grief, the deeper her devotion—at least, that was what Marcus believed.

So when Miriam finally found hope and slowly emerged from the dark pit, Marcus mistakenly assumed that his mother was forsaking his father's memory. Father, you'll never slip from my heart, he vowed. From that point forth, he balked whenever Miriam opened her home to her new friends. If he couldn't let go and move on, why should she?

Marcus was further incensed when his mother sold three

orchards to support the Teacher's work. That money belonged to his father and was to be handed down to Marcus. This was his inheritance. His father had worked hard to build this business, and he wouldn't have squandered it on a stranger who went against the Jewish establishment.

Now the Teacher was gone. Good riddance! Marcus sulked. Let mother weep over Him all she wants. At least we don't have to give away any more money. Let the disciples take care of themselves!

"LOOK OUT! Watch where you're going!"

The cobblestone streets of the Upper City were dark and, in his hurry to get home, Marcus ran headfirst into a group of stragglers. They wore the plain clothing of common laborers.

"Sorry—I wasn't looking," Marcus apologized.

"Don't you know it's the Sabbath?" the stranger asked. "Shouldn't you be home by now, with your family?"

Marcus stood silent. Something wasn't right. While most everyone else was scurrying about with their last-minute preparations, these men were just loafing in the street.

"My family isn't home right now, but that's where I'm headed."

"You're the son of Miriam, the olive merchant—aren't you?"

"She's not an olive merchant," Marcus retorted. "She's the owner of the groves. She has others who merchandise the olives and the oil. That's none of your business, anyhow!"

From behind him, Marcus felt a pair of strong hands seize his arms.

"What's going on?" protested Marcus. "Let me go! You have no—"

Marcus stopped mid-sentence after glancing down at the beefy hands that held his spindly arms and seeing the leather wristbands with the temple insignia on them. The guards (soldiers of the temple) had been hiding in the shadows. With their breastplates and helmets of brass, they served as body-guards to the high priest and those in his closest circle. They also served to keep order in the temple courts, particularly during Passover week.

"We have every right to detain Sabbath offenders," said the one who seemed to be a leader. "All transgressors are to be arrested and brought before the Council."

FOUR BLOCKS away, several members of the society of Pharisees reclined at a low table, dining on an assortment of boiled vegetables and cereals. The day had been long, and few of them had gotten any sleep in the past 24 hours. Although fatigued, they still had the energy to gloat about the remarkable turn of events that began the night before.

"It's been quite a successful Passover," remarked Abiel, his mouth still half-full from his last bite of salted fish. "Lots of Pascal lambs sacrificed. Plenty of commission made off of the money changers."

Abiel was a fat little chaber, highly ambitious, yet impulsive. As a chaber, he was a ranking member of the religious society. There were varying degrees of Pharisees within the society—from the novice to the more advanced chasid, or "pietist."

"Yes, everybody's happy. Everybody!" gloated Potiphera in a deep voice from the end of the table. He was among the highest-ranking members of the Sanhedrin, second only to the high priest. Normally he was grim, with a stern countenance that matched his authority. But tonight he was unusually spirited. His large belly shook as he slapped the table and whooped, "We even got rid of that Nazarene. 'King of the Jews'? More like 'King of the Pigs'!"

Howling, the men slapped one another and reveled in a job

well done. Now they could rest. Their troubles were over. Their Sabbath had come, and their power was still intact.

"And on the first day of the week," bragged Abiel, pointing directly behind him, "we'll round up the others and bring them to justice, starting with this wretch."

Facing the wall, under the watchful eye of a temple guard, was one of the Nazarene's closest followers, bound in cords. About six hours earlier, Thaddaeus, Andrew and Thomas—all followers of the Teacher—had made their way toward the Water Gate on the southeast side of Jerusalem. Under orders from Herod, each city gate was staffed with extra security. While Roman soldiers and temple guards normally worked separately, today there was the unusual visible presence of both groups, working in close proximity.

As the three disciples approached the Water Gate, Andrew began to get nervous. Suddenly he darted from the gate area, back toward the city. His abrupt movement flagged the attention of the guards—leaving Thaddaeus and Thomas alone and exposed.

Thaddaeus was the largest of the disciples. He was very muscular—barrel-chested, with brawny arms. With all the pent-up frustration and grief he felt from the Teacher's arrest and execution, this was not the day to tangle with Thaddaeus. As the guards turned toward him, something snapped. Instead of running from the guards, Thaddaeus charged them. It was an all out war.

Amazed, Thomas just stood and watched the scene. What a beast! He had never seen Thaddaeus in such a brawl.

Suddenly, Thomas felt the strong arms of a guard seize him. The man dragged him away from the crowds, slamming his small, bony frame against the south wall.

Curious onlookers flocked to the scene. A guard screamed out orders. In the pandemonium, Thomas struggled to keep an eye on Thaddaeus. The boisterous crowd was actually cheering Thaddaeus on, who was outnumbered five to one.

Using all his strength, Thaddaeus squirmed out from beneath the soldiers who had piled on top of him. His elbows thrust backward, knocking the wind out of one guard. Swinging wildly, his fists collided with the nose of another.

Casting the guards off like rag dolls, Thaddaeus freed himself and escaped northward, past the Valley Gate and back toward the temple area. Without looking back, he mistakenly assumed that Thomas had already escaped and had met up with Andrew. Instead, Thomas remained behind, still pinned against the wall, in fear for his life.

THROUGHOUT THE interrogation by the religious leaders, Thomas refused to disclose anything about the whereabouts of the remaining disciples. In response to their endless questions, Thomas just repeated, "They're all scattered. I can't tell you where anyone is."

"I think he can tell us," Potiphera said to Abiel. "He's just having trouble remembering. It's the Sabbath. Perhaps his mind should rest—and his stomach, too. When he gets hungry enough, then he'll remember."

As the day grew late, three other members of the Pharisaic society arrived. Each took turns interrogating Thomas.

The door opened abruptly and three more associates barged into the room. Pinned between two temple guards was Marcus.

"Well, look what we have here," mused Abiel. "Another catch?"

Marcus now realized that he was at the home of a high-ranking Sanhedrin official. Usually religious leaders were cloaked in mantles and temple vestments so they could be easily identified. Tonight, however, they were not so conspicuous. That's why Marcus hadn't recognized them when he stumbled upon them in the Upper City. Even Potiphera was dressed ostentatiously meek—betraying his position and power in Jewish society.

"It's the son of Miriam," announced one of the men. "He was wandering the streets. He says he was heading home—obviously breaking the Sabbath. He may be able to give us more information on the other followers of the Nazarene."

Marcus glanced over at Thomas, surprised that he, too, had been captured. Trying to go unnoticed, Thomas glared at him and wagged his head, silently warning, *Keep your mouth shut.*

Of course, Marcus wasn't about to talk. While he cared little about the disciples, he held the Jewish leaders in greater contempt. This was just one more opportunity to assert rebellious defiance.

"Talk, young man. What do you know of them? Where are they?"

"I don't know who you're asking about," Marcus lied.

SMACK! Abiel backhanded Marcus across the face.

"Don't be stupid. You can go free tonight if you just tell us where the followers of the Nazarene are hiding." As Abiel continued the interrogation, Potiphera left the room.

Marcus was determined not to give them anything. He knew the Pharisees were manipulative liars. Even if he told them everything they wanted to hear, it was still unlikely they'd release him.

"The Nazarene is dead," Abiel ranted. "It's all over. Talk to us."

Unbending, Marcus glared into the face of his interrogator, enjoying the challenge.

"You know where the followers are, don't you?"

Marcus didn't flinch.

Striking Marcus from behind, Abiel called out to the other religious leaders, "This one's pig-headed. Perhaps we need to visit his mother." Then turning to Marcus, Abiel gibed, "She's a supporter, isn't she?"

Marcus stiffened nervously, crossing his arms.

From an adjoining room, Potiphera returned, holding a garment in his hand. He tossed it on the table in front of Marcus.

"Explain this!" Potiphera railed, his face just inches from Marcus. "What about this sadin?" (A sadin is a linen cloth or wrapper, usually white, used as a nightshirt.)

"What about it, you goat?"

"It's evidence! Hard evidence against you!"

"What are you talking about?" asked Marcus, worried now.

Potiphera crossed his arms and sat down confidently, casting Marcus a dubious look.

"You've got to believe me," said Marcus. "I wasn't th—"

Mid-sentence, Marcus caught himself. He had slipped. Too much, you idiot. Be quiet!

"Wasn't . . . what?" Potiphera had caught it. "Wasn't there? Is that it, boy?"

Marcus was frozen.

"Spit it out. Just where weren't you?"

"I don't know what you're talking about," Marcus countered, trying to appear confident.

"Liar!" shouted Abiel.

Potiphera motioned Abiel to restrain himself. He knew they had the upper hand now.

"You were at Gethsemane. In the garden. At the time of the arrest. You were the mysterious young man that fled from our guards, weren't you?" Potiphera said, his voice calm.

"Don't worry. We won't hurt you. Just be honest with us."

Like a vulture orbiting its wounded, Potiphera quietly circled behind Marcus.

"It's yours, isn't it?" whispered Potiphera in his ear.

Marcus trembled. He fixed his gaze on Thomas, searching for help.

"Admit it. The sadin links you to the Nazarene," said Abiel.

Marcus shook his head in denial.

Potiphera slammed his fist down. "You were with the Nazarene, weren't you?"

Marcus still didn't budge.

"Open your mouth and speak, man. Tell us now," he said and then pointed to Thomas, "or you'll suffer the same fate that will befall this one."

In the tense moments of silence that followed, something happened that changed Marcus' demeanor. Abruptly, Marcus turned his gaze back toward his interrogators and smiled steadily.

"What is it now? A change of heart?"

"You fat-headed imbeciles think you're so clever, don't you? Is that all you're concerned about—the disciples' whereabouts?" he asked.

Marcus was baiting them.

"Tell us," said Potiphera, leaning closer. "What is it that you know?"

"If it's no concern to you, I guess it's no concern to me." Marcus taunted, "I wouldn't want to trouble you. Obviously, you have enough on your minds already."

"The teacher is dead," Abiel said testily. "What more is there to worry about?"

Marcus sat back, now confident. "Let's strike a bargain: I'll tell you what more there is to worry about if you promise to let Thomas and me go free."

Shaking his head in disbelief, Thomas was now just as confused as the Pharisees. What could Marcus possibly have up his sleeve?

PRISON BOOK PROJECT
P.O. Box 1146
Sharpes, FL 32959

67

"How can we trust you?" asked Potiphera. "Why should we let you go?"

"This is what we'll do," instructed Marcus, smirking, glancing at Thomas and then back at Potiphera. "Take us to Pilate. Hold us in custody there."

The Pharisees were confused.

Thomas was beside himself. Go to Pilate? Under the custody of the religious leaders? *Are you crazy?* That was the last thing Thomas wanted to do. *That's what happened to Jesus.*

Marcus continued, "Take us there and hold us until you learn that what I'm about to tell you is true and you get the permission you need."

"Permission we need? To do what? What information is of such worth as to merit your freedom?"

"First, agree to our freedom," pressed Marcus.

With that, Potiphera pulled Abiel and the other Pharisees aside.

Moments later, breaking from their huddle, Potiphera crouched low and stared Marcus down.

"Talk. Now!"

"First, you must—"

"Agreed, agreed!" Potiphera was clearly annoyed. "Now talk to us!"

Marcus leaned forward. "The corpse of the Teacher is in the hands of His secret disciples. It's being buried in a cave as we speak!"

"So? How does that concern us?" asked Potiphera. "He's dead. He's no longer a menace."

Marcus continued, "Pilate gave permission for His body to be given to these disciples! One is Yoseph of Arimathea and the other is Nicodemus."

Abiel pulled Potiphera aside, whispering frantically. Irritated, Potiphera brushed him off.

"Yoseph has never been a problem for us," Potiphera said.

"He would not oppose us. Nicodemus has always been inquisitive, but we can assure you that he is loyal to our society. We're only concerned about the most loyal followers of the Nazarene. They're the most troublesome ones. If you have no information on their whereabouts, then we're done talking."

"But wait," Marcus insisted, "you said that—"

"We promised you nothing."

"But—" Marcus was speechless with disbelief.

Abiel laughed. "Young man, you might as well settle in for a long night!"

"You thickheaded Pharisees!" Marcus spat back angrily. "Don't you get it? It's not about Yoseph or Nicodemus. It's about the corpse. It's out there. Unsecured. The followers have it."

"Who cares about a corpse? Let them bury it. The Nazarene is dead. He can't trouble us now!"

Marcus gazed at him. "So you're sure the Nazarene is dead?"

"That's absurd. Of course He's dead! Several members from the society witnessed the execution. We saw Him breathe His last and then rot for another three hours. When they finally smashed the legs of the two other thieves, the Nazarene was already dead."

Marcus was smiling now. "So you're convinced He's dead?"

"He's dead!" repeated Abiel, more heated now.

"He may have just fainted. How can you be certain He's really dead?" pressed Marcus.

"The lance pierced His side," Abiel said. "Blood and water flowed from His side. It was separated. There's no question He's dead!"

But Abiel was beginning to look worried. He glanced around at his fellow Pharisees for support.

"So what happens if His body comes up missing?" taunted

Marcus. "What if the disciples take His body away and hide it? What if they later insist that they saw Him alive?"

Abiel was now clearly flustered. "So what if one or two of the disciples say they saw Him alive? Who would be fooled by such a wild tale? Besides, they're all afraid and in seclusion. They couldn't pull off such a hoax. And even if they tried, none of them are smart enough to make it look convincing!"

"Hold on a moment, Abiel," said Potiphera, raising his hand. "The boy does have a point. The Nazarene did make remarks suggesting that He might rise from the dead."

Abiel frowned, confused.

"Indeed, the disciples are in disarray. Nevertheless, suppose they attempted this hoax? For a moment, let's suppose they secretly bury the Nazarene and then later champion the notion that He's alive. . ."

Potiphera sat down and studied Marcus.

"If Pilate has the authority to grant custody of the body to the disciples," he mulled, stroking his beard, "he also has the authority to grant protection to the tomb, against thieves and predators, of course. Follow me, Abiel?"

"So, we'll go to Pilate!" announced Abiel. "We'll get some sort of authority to secure the tomb—just in case!"

"Potiphera, that's a brilliant idea," cheered one of the other Pharisees.

But that was my idea! Abiel cast him a begrudging glance.

"Of course!" Potiphera accepted the accolade. "That's why the high priest appointed me to be second only to himself on the Sanhedrin."

"And what about our two prisoners?" questioned Abiel.

"We take them with us. They'll wait outside at Pilate's house. If the young man's statement is false, we bring them back and, after the Sabbath, prosecute them as insurrectionists. But if his report is true, we honor our oath and set them free."

"The Nazarene won't come back to life. That's ludicrous. Dead people stay dead!" sputtered Abiel.

"Abiel, don't worry. This is just insurance against any further problems," assured Potiphera. "We won't permit any rumor to begin about the Nazarene. His grave will be carefully guarded."

"Then let's make haste. We wouldn't want the Nazarene to already be risen, now, would we?" cackled Abiel, waving his hands and bowing in mock homage. "If that happened, surely our faith would be in vain."

SIX

THE FURTHER they marched, the more distracted Miriam became. During the long advance to the tomb, she was determined to give Mary her undivided attention. However, she was so curious about the conversation taking place behind the funeral bier that she couldn't help but eavesdrop on the two from the Sanhedrin.

Listening to the men, Miriam was surprised to hear them mutually share their testimonies about the Nazarene. As annoying as they were, both seemed to be genuine in their words and sincere in their intentions. By the time everyone arrived at the garden just north of Jerusalem, Miriam's suspicions of the two had eased enough to allow them to participate, in part, in the more physically demanding details of the burial preparations.

By now the sun was ebbing closer to the horizon. The long shadows cast over the rocky cliff on the garden's western edge created a dreary, gray backdrop.

At the grave's entrance, the soldiers were too large to fit through the opening with the corpse. Neither could the women carry in the corpse, at least not without Mary's help; and Miriam wasn't about to ask Mary to help with the limp and lifeless body of her son. That's when Miriam turned to Yoseph and Nicodemus. She assumed charge and ordered the two men to move the corpse into the tomb.

"Just get Him in there. And be careful!" she said, rather

testily. "The other women and I will take it from there." From the narrow entryway of the rock tomb, the women watched nervously and waited.

Nicodemus was the first to enter, smelling the mildewy air in the damp and musty cave. It was a natural cave that had been excavated and hewn out to form the sepulcher.

The back and side walls each had two shafts running parallel to each other to form six chambers. Each chamber had a smooth slab designed to hold a corpse. The bodies would lay with their feet toward the inner chamber with stone pillows for the heads at the far end.

Yoseph explained to Nicodemus that this corpse would be the first to occupy the cave. The tomb that he had personally saved for himself and his family was in Arimathea. Nevertheless, this was a first-rate tomb located in a prime location. He had purchased it seven years before as an investment.

"Make haste. The sun is setting!" snapped Miriam, sticking her head through the entrance.

Although Yoseph was happy to assist in the preparations, he was growing weary of Miriam's bossiness. Nicodemus raised his finger to pursed lips, motioning for Yoseph to swallow his anger.

"One . . . two . . . three . . . lift!"

Stooping beneath the five-foot-high rock ceiling of the sepulcher, the counselor and the Pharisee hoisted the Teacher's body up and into one of the small tunnels. Very solemnly, as for a fallen comrade—whom both wished they had known better—the two gently placed the torso in its resting position.

After lingering for a few moments of reflection, Yoseph and Nicodemus came out of the tomb. Then Magdalene and Maria, the mother of Joses, entered to begin caring for the body.

Outside, Miriam and Mary waited quietly with the men. No sooner had Yoseph and Nicodemus emerged from the tomb than Miriam made it unmistakably clear to both men—even though Yoseph was the garden's owner—that she was in charge and would not tolerate any further talking. This tomb, this burial, this preparation, and this mother must be revered by their silence.

Inside the tomb, Magdalene and Maria were surprised by how little room there was for them to do their preparations; yet, neither complained. This was a tomb for the honored, not for the crucified. Common criminals weren't supposed to be buried like this.

No, this was a real sepulcher. It was secure, with no entrances except for the front tunnel. A large stone was propped outside the tomb so that, once rolled into position, the chamber would be sealed off from pests, predators and plundering thieves. Magdalene knew that Mary would take comfort in the fact that her son was being dignified with such a burial.

Stretching her arms into the walled chamber, Magdalene began to wash the body of Jesus. Patiently, Maria watched. There was only room in the cramped chamber to work one at a time. Nevertheless, each worked quickly, taking turns to complete their task.

In part, the reason they hurried was to keep the Sabbath. But, more importantly, their haste was a cathartic attempt to expunge an impossible wrong. For too long they had been silent. For too long their beloved Teacher had hung on the cross. Haste now, to do the right thing. Haste now, to lay Him to rest. Haste now, for the Lord of the Sabbath.

Quickly but circumspectly, Magdalene washed the dried blood from around the face, sides, arms, hands and feet of Jesus. With tenderness, she washed around the nail holes, outlining the jagged brims with a moistened cloth, gently swabbing just inside the recesses.

As she cleansed the nail wounds, she thought about the cruel nails that had been extracted from them. She also thought back to how Jesus had ministered to her less than a year earlier, and the seven demons that He had extracted from her life—demons once bent on mentally crucifying her. Now, she was free!

Outwardly, her scars would testify to the Master's power. Inwardly, the derangement left in the demons' wake would slowly heal.

For months, she had doubted whether she would ever be truly whole in terms of what her culture considered normal and balanced. Sometimes she wondered if she still heard voices or if they were merely echoes from the wreckage and debris of her sordid past. Nevertheless, the more she was around Jesus, the more stable she felt.

By touching the corpse and nail wounds, Magdalene knew that she had become ceremonially defiled. Nevertheless, as she proceeded in these preparations, she felt increasingly cleansed. More than ever, she realized that defilement did not come from objects that one touched outwardly; rather, defilement came from the depravities that one embraced inwardly.

Maria then took her turn in the preparations. From a satchel provided by Nicodemus, she pulled out a large scent box containing burial spices. Under the dim torchlight, she took note of the transparent-brown color of the myrrh. It had a gummy texture. Reaching two fingers into the box, she then swabbed the ointment onto the corpse. (Myrrh was a sap-like resin that seeps from certain trees found in Africa and Arabia and hardens onto the bark. Not only was the resin used in embalming, it was also a principle ingredient in the holy anointing oil of the Jews.)

Carefully, delicately, she rubbed the ointment onto the skin of the corpse and massaged it into the wounds. The putrid sweet odor that filled the chamber nearly overwhelmed the women.

Outside the tomb, Miriam and Mary also caught a strong

whiff of the myrrh. Mary thought back to the first time she had first smelled such an aroma. It was just after the birth of her son. Three royal strangers had traveled to where they were lodging. They claimed to have been directed by the heavens and came bearing very expensive gifts—gold, frankincense and myrrh. These were items that she and Joseph had never dreamed of owning and that they would later sell to finance their hasty flight to Egypt.

At the time, Mary had marveled at the splendor of the gold ornaments and the fragrance of the sweet-smelling incense. But she was taken aback by the gift of myrrh. Embalming ointment? Yet now, three decades later, the prophetic nature of that gift hit her.

After washing the body and anointing it with the perfumes, spices and aromatic ointments, Maria emerged from the chamber. She then nodded to the mother of Jesus that her work had been completed, and it was time for the final preparations to be made.

The burial blankets and wrappings that Miriam carried to the tomb were on the ground next to where Mary had been resting. With a loving nudge from Miriam, Mary picked up the linens and slowly proceeded into the tomb. The small torch near the entrance helped Mary as she scanned the chamber, inspecting its suitability for this occasion. The walls were roughly hewn and the ceiling low.

Inside, Magdalene took Mary by the arm and directed her toward the ledge upon which her son rested. Mary saw that the two women had done a marvelous job in the care of the corpse, bathing the flesh and anointing it with the gummy spices. Now it was her turn.

With apprehension, Mary commenced this most difficult task that was dreaded by every mother. With tears streaming, she began wrapping her son in the linens, as was the custom of the Jews. The grave bands were about a foot wide. Slowly and methodically, she banded His body. Then she covered His face and enshrouded it. Between the folds of the grave bands, she and Magdalene worked to apply additional layers of spices.

Just three short decades before, in a borrowed cave, she and her husband had first wrapped their son in similar linens; only that time they were the linens that were customary of the Jews at birth. After cutting the umbilical cord, her husband proudly washed their newborn son and rubbed Him down with salt, as was common in the care of a Hebrew baby. She then laid Him diagonally on a square piece of cloth. First one corner and then another were turned over His little body and feet. Finally, His whole body was wrapped with linen bands wound around the outside.

As she swaddled her baby, the cries of her infant subsided into soft whimpers and faint coos. Her newborn found a renewed sense of warmth and security in the womb-like cloths that restricted and contained His movement.

At the time, Mary had marveled how a boundless and everlasting God could be wrapped, bound, tied up, and contained in simple swaddling cloths. The omnipotent and sovereign God lay helpless as a newborn and in need of the warmth and security of a baby's blanket. Here, the everlasting God was now swaddled not just by simple linens, but also by human flesh, human emotions, and the fullness of the human experience.

One last time. Oh, to swaddle you, my baby.

Just to hold Him, just to contain Him, and just to protect Him one last time. Was this too much to ask?

When He was afraid of the night, she swaddled and assured Him by rocking Him. When He skinned an elbow, she swaddled and cheered Him with her healing kisses. When He was perturbed, she swaddled and calmed Him with her understanding embrace. When He was unrestrained in joyous exuberance, she swaddled and contained Him with her own excitement. Even when His earthly father—Joseph—died, she swaddled and consoled Him with her soothing tears.

Just one more time. Please?

The preparations were mostly complete now. The hour was late. Her son had been tended to. At her side, Magdalene could hear the soft whispers of a mother's benediction, "Good night, my son. Sleep well. . ."

Mary paused.

Then beaming through her tears, she added, "Morning is coming."

"MAKE HASTE! Secure the tomb!"

The utter stillness that had encompassed the garden cemetery was abruptly shattered by the gruff orders and blazing torches coming from the gated entrance. Intruders! Soldiers!

Maria, the mother of Joses, shrieked in fright. Nicodemus ran ahead to prevent the intrusion, but upon learning its source, was again beset by his old fears and timidity. Miriam just stood silent, shaking her head—annoyed at what was now one more disruption to the dignified burial she had tried so hard to manage.

Signaling that he would handle the intrusion, Yoseph of Arimathea marched angrily toward the front of the cemetery. This was his property and this was no time for trespassers.

"You are not welcome here!" insisted Yoseph, calling out to the silhouetted figures moving quickly in his direction.

"Step aside, Yoseph!" a command barked from behind the temple guards. "We have orders from Pilate."

Pilate?

It was Abiel the Pharisee, second in command to Potiphera.

"What do you mean?" Yoseph stood his ground. "I have orders from Pilate!" He waved the parchment that had been sealed by Pilate earlier that afternoon. "By decree of the procurator, I have been granted custody of the Nazarene's body. This is private property and you are trespassing."

Yoseph now regretted that he had sent the centurion and his men away just an hour earlier. Once they had carried the body to the garden, he assumed their services were no longer needed.

Abiel pulled out his own parchment, similar to the one that Yoseph was holding.

"Your custody ends once the Nazarene is in the tomb," said Abiel. "Pilate has given us this decree."

Yoseph studied the parchment. It stated that once the Nazarene was entombed, the grave was to be sealed and guarded to protect against thieves.

Brushing Yoseph aside, the guards proceeded through the garden and ahead to the torch-lit entrance of the cave.

Sheepishly, Nicodemus cowered behind Maria, holding her but also shielding himself. Standing at the tomb's entrance was Miriam, unmoved, staring angrily at the intruders. *I dare anyone to disturb this grave!*

"Well, well," smirked Abiel, "if it isn't Nicodemus."

Faltering, Nicodemus started to look away until his eyes caught Miriam's reproachful gaze.

Abiel continued in his derision. "Why doesn't this surprise me? Something told me that you were sympathetic to the Nazarene. How long has this been going on?"

In that moment, a change happened in Nicodemus. Before, he had wanted to run. Fear made it hard to breathe. Here was a high commander of the Pharisees standing before him with the temple guards. What would they do? What would the Sanhedrin say about him?

But now, unexpectedly, something snapped. In that dark moment, the same outrage that had erupted earlier at the execution site now bubbled once again. For just a moment, he felt a surge of courage. *I can do this!* he told himself.

Unfortunately for Nicodemus, however, his target was not alone.

Standing just behind the guards, Yoseph could see the anger rising up in Nicodemus. He furtively motioned to Nicodemus not to do anything rash.

But Abiel continued taunting and razzing him, baiting the fight.

Nicodemus clenched his fists tightly to his side. Adrenaline surged. He was cocked and ready. *This one's for the Teacher*, he seethed.

But when he darted forward from behind Maria and started to lunge, she caught his arm and jerked him back.

"No, Nicodemus! Don't do it!" cried Miriam.

From behind the guards, Yoseph rushed forward to assist Maria and Miriam in restraining Nicodemus. "You're a murderous dung heap, Abiel!" Nicodemus spit. "You and all the rest!"

"Whatever do you mean, Nicodemus?" jeered Abiel. "The stone you cast at us is, unfortunately, also the stone that comes back to hit you. The blood of the Nazarene is as much on your hands as it is on ours."

"You will not touch the Nazarene any further!" yelled Nicodemus. "Go away. Leave us alone!"

Abiel laughed and then folded both hands over his heart. "You misunderstand our purposes, dear Nicodemus. We have no intentions of touching the Nazarene." His syrupy words reeked of evil. "Becoming defiled by that rotting corpse is the last thing we would want. We just want to make certain that no one else touches Him."

With all the noise, Magdalene emerged from the tomb, followed by Mary. "What's happening out here?"

Abiel pulled out the parchment for Mary's inspection. On its edges were the waxy remnants of Pilate's signet.

"Our condolences to you," Abiel said with a sickly smile.

Mary silently glared at Abiel.

Abiel continued, "Madam, we mean no harm to your son. Indeed, we are here for His protection. We have orders from Pilate to ensure that no one disturbs the tomb. Your son will be guarded like a king. This tomb will be sealed against thieves that might otherwise plunder it."

Glancing over at Nicodemus and Yoseph, Abiel continued, "We have the greatest respect for the Nazarene, you know." He smiled wryly. "We wouldn't want anything to happen to Him."

Yoseph and Nicodemus stared at him in disbelief.

"Guards, secure the tomb!"

Upon Abiel's command, the guards moved everyone aside. Although he did not enter, for fear of ceremonial defilement, Abiel did peek just inside the tomb to be sure that the corpse was present. Once he was satisfied, he enjoined Mary to return home with her friends, assuring her that the burial cave would be properly closed, sealed, and guarded.

A SHORT TIME LATER, when they were out of the guards' sight, Mary and the others paused to observe the activity at the front of the tomb. Upon the orders of Abiel, the guards had sheathed their swords and stood at ease.

To Mary's relief, no one else entered the cave. She feared that once they had left, Abiel and the guards would do something to desecrate the tomb.

Soon, the guards moved to one side of the cave. Three of them levered a beam just under the base of the huge stone that would seal the entrance. The other guards gathered around the far edge of the stone. This large slab was similar to the big, bulky rocks quarried for ancient temple construction.

Combining their strength, the soldiers tugged, pushed and pried the huge stone. Bearing down with all their might, their efforts caused the blocking stone to start to wobble and then rock. With one final thrust, the large slab teetered, lurched, and then tumbled end-over-end in its narrow channel and downward in front of the tunnel entrance. The guards quickly backed away as the slab settled itself.

The tomb was now safeguarded against animals and thieves. To remove the slab would take up to three times the manpower it took to originally roll it into place.

Oddly, Mary's anger at Abiel's intrusion turned to private relief. While Abiel was concerned that the disciples might take the body, Mary was afraid that the religious leaders would be the ones to do so. Tonight, by virtue of mutual distrust, the body would be protected. No one would disturb her son. He would rest securely.

Still spying from a distance, Mary and her friends watched as a guard on one side of the stone held a torch while another carried a bar of wax to be melted onto the surface of the tomb wall. A third guard secured one end of the cord against the wall while the wax melted around it and against the rock. Once a big blob of wax was in place, still warm and tacky, the signet of Rome was embossed. Then the cord was wrapped across the blocking stone and stretched firmly to the other side where the wax insignia was again affixed.

The insignia on the waxy seals contained the imperial Roman seal. This emblem was like a badge, representing the authority of Rome. It was a grim warning not to disturb the grave. The seals were to be broken only with the approval of Pilate and the governing authorities.

Mary knew that it was with this insignia and these types of seals that most other binding edicts were issued. From the old books of Jewish history, she recalled when Daniel was imprisoned in a cave of lions. The cave was closed off by a large rock and sealed with the king's cords and insignia. It was a day or so later when the king returned. Daniel was alive and well, victoriously delivered by Yahweh God. This meditation buoyed her as she prepared to depart from the garden.

With the grave now sealed, the troops marched back and forth before the entrance. Positioned in two rows fanning out from the blocking stone, the guards formed a defensive perimeter surrounding the cave's entrance.

Magdalene and Maria walked away still trembling inside from all the turmoil and confusion. Nicodemus left feeling bitter at Abiel, but invigorated that at least he hadn't fled and had stood up to his associates. Yoseph walked away disappointed that his property had been invaded and that Pilate had issued a second decree that seemed, in part, to have reversed the earlier decree, and thus took matters out of his hands.

Miriam walked away still tense from her need to be in control. She had raced to manage everything she could in a day that was mostly unmanageable. Only after they had safely exited the garden, re-entered Jerusalem, passed through the Mishneh district, entered the Upper City and her neighborhood and, finally, her home, could Miriam dare to slow down. To show weakness or to succumb to grief was unacceptable in her eyes. She had to care for Mary. *Who else would?* she thought. Only after there was no one more to care for and nothing further to fix would she, herself, break under exhaustion.

Engulfed in motherly sorrow, Mary walked at Miriam's side. Her only comfort, besides her friends, was the seal on the tomb. Although she didn't like how it happened, she at least had the assurance that the burial cave was safeguarded.

For at least the next 30 hours or so, the corpse would, in fact, rest undisturbed. Standing at attention outside the cave, in the finest of military discipline, armed with shields and swords, the temple guards kept the sepulcher. Standing at attention within the chamber, in all their ethereal glory, armed with light and love, the celestial guards kept the Son.

SEVEN

THE SABBATH night seemed endless. However, it would have been much longer had Marcus' tale regarding the custodial transfer of the corpse not proven true. Fortunately, along with Thomas, he was allowed to go free. Upon their release, they headed straight to Marcus' house.

Thomas had been to the home of Miriam and Marcus many times in the past three years. The stucco house, with its walls inlaid with beams, had become the common meeting place for the disciples in Jerusalem. Eventually, this house would be sold and the proceeds bequeathed to the treasury of the early church.

After pounding on the door, a servant girl answered. She shrieked when she saw Thomas. Standing behind Thomas, just out of her view, was Marcus. Swiftly, the door slammed shut.

Inside the house, the word had been that Thomas was being held by the temple guard and would likely suffer the same horrible fate as Jesus. Seeing Thomas unexpectedly at the door was like seeing a ghost.

Marcus stepped forward to rap on the door. "Let us in!" shouted Marcus, knocking hard.

Just when Marcus was glancing back at Thomas, the door suddenly flew open. This time Thaddaeus was on the other side. From behind Thaddaeus, Andrew bolted to embrace Thomas in the doorway.

"Thomas, what are you doing here? Weren't you arrested? How did you escape?" Andrew asked eagerly. "We couldn't get to you. Are you all right?"

"What do you mean, 'We couldn't get to you?'" Thomas laughed. "You never tried. You ran away, Andrew! You left Thaddaeus and me behind."

Andrew dropped his head, ashamed.

Marcus scooted around him into the house. "Talk all you want, I'm hungry," he declared, hurrying toward the kitchen with the bread he had purchased.

"Andrew, it's all right," reassured Thomas. "We were all scared, weren't we? We all froze at the gate."

"What do you mean 'we'?" swaggered Thaddaeus. "By the time I was done with them, they were terrified of me!"

"That's right, Thaddaeus," Thomas burst out laughing, "you showed them what you were made of. They'll think twice before they tangle with you again!"

"Let's get inside," said Andrew. "Thomas, you must be hungry."

As Thaddaeus and Andrew closed the door, Thomas called for Marcus.

Marcus popped his head out of the kitchen. "What is it?"

"Save me some of that heart cake from Ammi's," said Thomas.

Thaddaeus raised his hand, "I'll take some, too!"

For the next hour, behind closed doors, Thomas, Andrew, Thaddaeus and the remaining disciples broke bread and reviewed the shocking events of the day.

EARLIER THAT day, before Jesus had been crucified, 10 of the disciples had assembled at the house of Miriam. Only Peter and Judas were missing. Their whereabouts were unknown. Everyone assumed the best—that the two men were together, safe, and secretly monitoring the proceedings against Jesus.

The remaining disciples stayed in seclusion inside Miriam's house. The windows of her house, like those of most homes, were small and latticed, providing sufficient privacy for those inside. Should the temple guards make a surprise visit, the disciples would scramble down into the storage granary under the floor. The cellar was mostly empty and was a perfect place to harbor fugitives, if necessary.

By the second hour of the day, however, everything had worsened for the disciples. Miriam had just arrived back from the hearings at Pilate's house. Her eyes were red and her manner dispirited.

She was immediately hit with one question after another about Jesus' fate.

"What did they say?"

"He will be freed, won't he?"

"Miriam, give us some good news!"

Ignoring the questions, she went directly to Mary and took her by the hand into the adjoining room. The disciples and other women started to follow, but Miriam shooed them all back, except for John, whom she motioned forward into the room.

From where the disciples and the other women waited, they could only hear the indistinguishable whispers of Miriam furtively talking to Mary. Deep within, they knew that whatever had happened, it was not good. Each waiting heart wanted to lunge from its breast—beating harder with each passing second—restrained only by the knowledge that this moment of privacy must be respected.

"No!"

A shrill cry came from the adjoining room.

"No!" It was now a wail. "Please . . . No! I must go and be with Him."

Rushing in from the other room, first the women and then the disciples surrounded the weeping mother. As the report of

Jesus' approaching fate rippled through the room, torrents of emotion were unleashed. Some gasped and choked; others stood silent, dumfounded and disbelieving. Some reacted violently, and struck the walls; others lay prostrate, faint with grief.

As Miriam cradled Mary, she motioned Thomas to draw closer. "You must leave here immediately!" she instructed. "Jerusalem is no longer safe. What has befallen the Master can happen to you and the others as well. I will take Mary to Golgotha, and John has agreed to accompany us. The rest of you should leave right now."

"But what about Peter and Judas?" Thomas asked.

"They're not here?" Miriam asked, searching the room.

Indeed, they were absent. None of the disciples had seen them since Jesus' arrest.

Miriam was annoyed by Thomas' hesitant manner and endless questions. She felt overwhelmed just trying to help Mary, as well as absorbing all the other grief that had swept the room. But she bit her tongue and proceeded to brief Thomas on everything that she had seen and witnessed at Pilate's court. She hadn't seen Judas at all. As for Peter, the last time she had seen him was shortly after the arrest the night before, and that was only at the courtyard near the high priest's house. By now, both Judas and Peter should have returned to the house to meet with the rest of the disciples.

"You must go now!" admonished Miriam. "Make haste. Only John will remain behind with us. Leave Jerusalem now!"

Upon her urging, Thomas convened the other nine disciples. They conceded that Miriam was right and that they should depart immediately. Judas and Peter had likely been arrested by the temple guards and would suffer the same fate as their Master was about to suffer. This shared fate would be theirs, too, if they didn't immediately follow Miriam's counsel.

The remaining disciples divided themselves into groups. Attempting to exit Jerusalem in one group, let alone walk down the streets together, would be too conspicuous. Instead, they broke up into four small bands. This would arouse less suspicion. The groups would then exit Jerusalem by different gates. Once outside, they would rendezvous in Bethany at the house of Lazarus.

However, even with the coordinated efforts to escape detection, only Phillip, Bartholomew, and James the son of Alphaeus actually made it safely to Bethany. Matthew and Simon (the Zealot) aborted the plan when they saw how heavily guarded the Sheep Gate was. The threesome of Andrew, Thomas, and Thaddaeus came unraveled at the Water Gate, with Thomas being detained.

James was to wait for his brother John to arrive back from Golgotha and then flee together. However, before John had a chance to return, Andrew and Thaddaeus had already stumbled back to Miriam's house to warn James of the danger. A short time later, Matthew and Simon also retreated to the house and corroborated the danger. Once Jesus had breathed His last, Mary released John to hurry back to Miriam's house and meet up with his brother.

IN THE late evening hours of that dreadful Friday, the seven disciples that remained in Jerusalem took inventory of the terrible events that had passed. Three of the disciples were presumed safe in Bethany. Still missing were Peter and Judas. Thankfully, Thomas was home safe. With his escape from the religious leaders, the disciples had hoped that Thomas might have something to report on the whereabouts of Peter and Judas, but he hadn't seen either of them.

Matthew and John speculated that Peter and Judas had likely fled and were safely away from Jerusalem. Thaddaeus countered that they would have at least left word with someone regarding their intentions. The others feared that the pair might have been captured. Thomas reminded them, however, that when he and Marcus were detained, there was no sign of either. In fact, Abiel and Potiphera had never even mentioned their names.

As the seven disciples talked about the fate of their two missing friends, a series of forceful knocks came on the entry door. These knocks were not random but seemingly in coded succession.

"It's Miriam!" announced the servant girl excitedly.

As she opened the door, Miriam, along with Magdalene and Mary, bustled in. For the remainder of the evening, the seven disciples loitered about the house. In the kitchen area, Miriam distracted Magdalene with an assortment of duties.

In the main room, the disciples took turns consoling Mary. Their efforts to assuage her grief, however, were futile. Her sorrow was not ready to be disarmed; silence would have been preferred. Instead of calming the mother with supportive presence, the room was quickly charged with cathartic grandstanding.

First, James blamed himself, followed by Simon. Each disciple in turn impugned himself in a manner that became increasingly self-deprecating—each competing to atone for themselves with Mary. Andrew then pulled Mary aside and explained how it was he who had tried to warn her son not to come to Jerusalem. Then Matthew chimed in, countering that it was he, not Andrew, who had warned the Master.

As the war of egos ensued, Miriam finally got fed up.

Storming into the room, she yelled, "Get out! All of you! The hour is late!"

"What——?" Thaddaeus stared at her, startled.

"Open that foolhardy trap one more time and I'll fill it with this dish rag!" thundered Miriam. This was her house and her friend. The evil of this day would not be further overshadowed by the disciples' virile rivalry.

Miriam continued, "We're all upset and you're only making things worse. Go upstairs and sleep it off!"

Driven out by Miriam, the disciples quickly shuffled up the outside stairs to the roof. The roof on Miriam's house was flat, like that of most dwellings. Small timbers were spaced evenly on top and covered with brush and wood, then covered with a compacted layer of mud mixed with chopped straw. On top of the roof was a roller stone that was used to periodically re-compact and harden the roof so that rain would not seep through. This upper chamber was also furnished with a low table and plenty of blankets for lounging. Miriam's loft served as a place of amusement, business, conversation, and even wor-ship at times. In the cool of the evening, it served as place to retreat from the narrow, filthy streets below.

"What's gotten into her? We were just trying to help," James asked Thaddaeus.

"She's had a rough day."

"That's an understatement," Simon piped in. "Haven't we all had a rough day?"

Thaddaeus rolled his eyes, "If you two hadn't been so stupid, we'd still be down below where it's warm. Thanks to you, we get to wake up with cold dew on our beards."

"What do you mean 'stupid'?"

"Don't you get it?" lectured Thomas, "Mary just lost her son and ——"

"——and we just lost the Master," interrupted Thaddaeus. "James, that was no time for you to claim you tried to warn the Master. You might just as well blame His execution on the rest of us!"

"At least I tried," said James. "That's more than you did!" He started to walk away, but then turned and fired back, "Don't forget, Thaddaeus, that it was you who encouraged the Master to come to Jerusalem."

That did it. Thaddaeus rushed toward James and shoved

him backwards, then grabbed him and held him by the shoulders, halfway over the balcony edge. James was no match for Thaddaeus. Furious, John leaped onto Thaddaeus, then Simon joined the mellee as well, releasing his own pent-up resentment against James and John, who had made their self-aggrandizing remarks a week earlier. *Sit at the Master's right and left? I don't think so!*

Miriam came storming up the stairs.

Clanging a brass plate, she first smashed it against the head of Simon, and then against each of the others. They quickly retreated.

"This is the last time I'm going to say this" she hissed, shaking her bony finger. "It's been a long day. We're all tired. And Mary needs her rest!"

She swiveled her head from side to side, glaring at the disciples.

"This is my house," she continued, "and I'm exhausted. Any more of your foolish deviltry and I'll personally fetch the temple guards to haul you each away. Do I make myself clear?"

Chastened, the disciples quickly nodded, hanging their heads in shame.

"Now go to sleep!" she growled one last time, descending the stairs. "Not one more word!"

EIGHT

IT SEEMED like it was only an hour later, and yet it was already almost dawn when Thomas was awakened.

"Thomas get up!" whispered Marcus as he roused the disciple awake.

"Shhh—leave me alone."

"Wake up," Marcus persisted. "There's something you've got to see."

Thomas grumbled dopily, rolling over in his blanket. *I just got to sleep.* Actually, he had been asleep for over two hours and soon it would be daybreak.

"Go to bed already!" groaned Thomas.

"You must get up!" insisted Marcus. "It can't wait."

Thomas turned back over, stupefied. Propping himself up, he looked around. *No one else is awake, why am I?* The other six disciples were still fast asleep. Dogs barking in distant homes were the only noises on this pre-dawn Sabbath morning.

"Are any of the women awake down below?" moaned Thomas.

"No. It's just me."

"What's so important, Marcus?"

"I think I might just know where Judas is."

"What?" said Thomas, rubbing the sleep from his eyes—his brain slowly cranking into gear.

Judas . . . that's right . . . he's still missing, isn't he?

Thomas yawned widely. "Is he all right? Is Peter with him?"

"Shhh—keep it down," Marcus instructed Thomas. "And no, Peter is not with him. Now let's go."

"What about the temple guards?" asked Thomas.

"He's alone, but we need to go to him!"

For the moment, Thomas was too groggy to ask any more questions. He hurriedly dressed, put on his sandals and followed Marcus down the stairs and onto the cobblestone street below.

The two hurried eastward through the Upper City to the stairway leading downward into the Lower City of Jerusalem. Before descending the stairs, they noticed in the distance a squad of guards heading in their direction.

Because the early morning fog had settled down into the Lower City, it was unlikely that Thomas and Marcus had been spotted; but just in case, they hid themselves around the back edge of the aqueduct. This elevated section of the stone and masonry water channel snaked through the city from the Serpent's Pool just east of Jerusalem to the interior of the city and as far as the temple. Behind the aqueduct, near the stairs, they waited for the soldiers to pass by.

These guards had just been relieved at the southwest gate of Jerusalem. Originally, the military watches of the night had been three in number, but the Romans introduced an additional watch to make it four: the evening, midnight, cock-crowing, and morning watch. Military watches were typically posted on the city walls, at the gates, on the streets, and at strategic points of interest. Retiring to their homes, the eight guards dragged themselves up the narrow stairs and paused to recount the night, before scattering in different directions.

Concealed deep within the shadows of the aqueduct, Thomas and Marcus listened intently. At first, it seemed as though one of the guards may have spotted them, but instead of checking it out further, the guard nervously moved away from the shadows and quickly back toward the group. The other soldiers glanced over toward the aqueduct and then cackled, making sport of the guard.

Some of the guards spoke of last night's watch as being especially creepy. Perhaps it was the dense, grey fog that enveloped the city. Maybe it was the moaning of the wind. Whatever it was, something terribly unearthly had occurred that evening, leaving many of them unnerved.

One ornery guard taunted the others. "Something ghostly! Something haunting!" he jabbed.

Ghosts? wondered Marcus.

The guard mentioned that there was a rumor of emptied tombs in the aftermath of the previous day's earthquake. As the guards tattled and teased, even Thomas and Marcus started feeling uneasy. Reference was also made to the guarded tomb of the Nazarene, making it at least one less corpse to be numbered among the phantasm.

Perhaps their ungoverned imaginations had run amuck—at least Thomas hoped so. A few lingering earth tremors, along with the darkness of the morning hour, the dense fog, and an eerie breeze all coalesced to bedevil the bravest of soldiers.

"The next watch better stay vigilant," one guard howled, slapping another on the back as he waved goodnight. He winked. "They, too, may have some unexpected company before daybreak!"

Thomas and Marcus wondered if the guards were referring to them. Did they know the two were hiding in the shadows of the aqueduct? *Maybe they're baiting us,* thought Marcus. *But what, exactly, are the guards so worried about, anyway?*

As the squad split up and strolled out of sight, Thomas and Marcus snuck down the stairs leading into the Lower City and continued to follow the aqueduct toward the Essene Gate. The predawn fog that had enveloped the city loomed low and mysteriously heavy now. The dusty brown tint of the city walls and stucco houses now appeared grey and gloomy. The walls extending out from the city gate on either side were only visible for 20 feet at the most and then were enveloped by the haze.

As for the Essene gate, it was guarded, but not as heavily as the day before. During the crucifixion, a regiment of 16 guards had been assigned to each gate—all Roman soldiers.

After the first watch of the night, these soldiers were replaced with auxiliary, non-citizen guards—the local militia who were under the command of the city council. These crusty guards paled in comparison to the polished Roman soldiers and temple guards. Their equipment was crude, their uniforms tattered, and their discipline lax. Nevertheless, the watchmen were sufficiently prepared to quickly signal for backup in the event that an enemy approached the city walls.

Sizing up the ragtag troops, Marcus felt more optimistic that they could make it through the gates without being detained. Marcus could have done so easily. His concern was for Thomas.

"We can do this," whispered Marcus.

Thomas shook his head. "What if they recognize me?"

"This isn't like it was yesterday," urged Marcus. "It's dark and hazy. They'll let us pass."

But Thomas was reluctant. Was his name still on the most-wanted list? Were the authorities still looking for the disciples? What would happen if they were detained again? Thomas marveled how Philip, Bartholomew and James the son of Alphaeus had managed to slip out of Jerusalem earlier—assuming they actually did.

Judas! I must not forget poor Judas. He needs us. Courage now.

As the pair talked quietly, Marcus finally came up with a plan. He would remain hidden behind the aqueduct near the gate. Thomas would double back 100 feet and then cut around the houses. From a clothesline, Thomas would snatch a sheet and then position himself behind a dwelling closest to the opposite side of the gate. Marcus would then create a diversion. With the guards distracted, Thomas could dart through the gate, disguised by the linen covering his head.

Hidden in the cold shadows and arrayed in a borrowed linen, Thomas waited nervously. He could feel his heart racing. *Can we really pull this off?* It was just yesterday that Andrew, Thaddaeus and he had been spotted trying to leave Jerusalem. He remembered how it felt watching Andrew duck and run, seeing Thaddaeus fighting the guards, and feeling his own back explode in pain as he was slammed against the city wall.

This morning would be different. *It has to be different! Judas needs our help.* Marcus and Thomas had to get to him. On this sleepy pre-dawn morning, the militia was not as alert. They milled about, rather detached from their job, jesting with one another.

Suddenly, Thomas heard a ghastly noise. *What was that?* He looked around. Silence. The soldiers stood frozen. Then another chilling howl came from the shadows across from him.

That can't be Marcus, can it? Thomas wondered.

Frightened, Thomas froze as well, unable to move, except for an involuntary twitch of his eyelid and the quiver of his hand. The chilly breeze picked up, stiff now—the fog thickening even more.

Quickly the guards unsheathed their swords. Nervously, they circled about with their backs to one another. Each pointed and nudged the others toward the shadows where Marcus had been hiding. As Thomas watched, he feared for Marcus, but it was readily apparent that none of the guards were willing to broach the darkness and confront the uncanny specter.

Again, another subhuman sound. This time a deep, phlegmatic moan resonated among the dwellings.

Thomas' heart raced wildly. Without further thought, he slipped from behind the house and bolted through the gate.

Two of the guards noticed the darting motion peripherally, but in the haze it was merely a fleeting blur—probably from yet one more unidentified phantom, they reasoned.

Outside the gate and hidden next to the wall, Thomas bent over to catch his breath.

Inside the gate and still concealed behind the aqueduct, Marcus waited in amusement. *Just stay put, Thomas. I'm not far behind.*

Eventually the guards turned from the aqueduct and back toward the gate. Marcus then crept slowly backwards and up the street until he was out of their range.

Behind one of the dwellings, a large basket of rubbish had been set outside, readied for a trip to the Hinnom dump after the Sabbath. Marcus picked it up, circled around some flats, and then carried it nonchalantly down the middle of the street toward the gate, in full view.

"Halt right there," a soldier growled. "It's the Sabbath. You wouldn't want the temple guards seeing you with that load."

"I need to pass through the gate."

"Not at this hour, young man."

Marcus was prepared. Cunningly, he dropped the large basket of rubbish in the street, spilling its contents. He then pulled 25 copper coins from his pocket and held them out. When the lead watchman reached for the coins, Marcus retracted his fist and took five steps away from the mess in front of the gate.

"I'm sure the Council wouldn't want any Passover pilgrims to see our beautiful streets filled with such rubbish," chided Marcus, "now would they?"

The watchman looked at him, dumfounded.

"Would they?" persisted Marcus, again holding out the

coins, only this time nodding to the lead guard that he'd better take them.

Flustered, the watchman reached out and took the coins. He then barked, "You will clean up this waste and remove it from the city, immediately!"

Quickly, Marcus scooped the waste into the basket and scooted out through the gate. Marcus snickered under his breath, *And these are the fierce defenders of Jerusalem?*

Although the early morning sun was beginning to slice through the fog, it was still difficult to see more than 30 feet in any direction. From behind him, Marcus felt strong hands grab his shoulders.

Startled, Marcus whirled around. *Cursed soldiers!*

"We made it!"

It was Thomas, grinning from ear to ear.

"Don't ever do that again!" said Marcus, catching his breath.

"But we made it out, Marcus. We're all right!"

"Quiet!" warned Marcus, trying to restrain Thomas. They were still not out of range of the watchmen.

Further down the path, Marcus finally let Thomas revel in their successful escape.

"That was clever. How did you do that?"

"Promise you won't tell anyone?" said Marcus.

"I promise!"

"I've had a lot of practice, but you mustn't tell anyone about it."

"You can trust me," said Thomas.

"Mother had a merchant friend who was a soothsayer," boasted Marcus. "The woman became wealthy by getting the dead to belch out the fortunes of anyone who would pay for it."

The Mosaic law expressly forbade such wizardry and divination. Necromancy (the heathen practice of conjuring up the dead by magic to tell future events) was punishable by death. Of course, the dead could never really be beseeched. It was all trickery. The deceptive art was forbidden because it unwittingly exploited people who were superstitious. Yahweh God wanted His people to trust in Him rather than in necromantic trickery.

"But how did you make such a sound?" asked Thomas.

"It's easy! Imagine putting your mouth to the rim of a hollow ceramic pot or leather water bottle and speaking into it. It makes a low murmuring sound."

Thomas tipped his head, puzzled.

Marcus continued, "In the same way, a soothsayer speaks gutturally from the belly and throws her voice. The good ones can do it without moving their lips, making it appear that someone else is talking."

Thomas marveled.

"Think about it," said Marcus. "Why do most soothsayers work in the dark by candlelight?"

"So they won't be incriminated?" Thomas replied.

"That, and also because most of them are not that skilled. They don't want paying customers seeing their lips move. It's all an illusion, you know."

"Still, the law strictly forbids it!" said Thomas.

Marcus laughed. "But you have to admit, the illusion did fool the guards back there!"

"It almost worked on me as well," said Thomas.

"It works on Magda—" Marcus slipped.

Thomas stopped in his path. "What?"

Marcus had been caught. Curses rang in his head.

"Never mind, Thomas," said Marcus nervously, waving him off.

"It works on who?" Thomas wouldn't let it go. "Who else have you been messing with?"

Marcus dropped his head.

"Come on, Marcus—tell me."

"All right," Marcus swallowed. "Magdalene."

Thomas slowly shook his head in disbelief.

"Magdalene!" Marcus repeated indignantly. "Are you happy now? I said it! It was Magdalene!"

Thomas was visibly shocked.

"The girl once had seven spirits," Marcus defended, holding up one hand and then the other, extending his fingers one at a time. "Count them . . . Seven! You know she's a little crazy. She was already used to hearing voices in her head. And with my help, sometimes she still does."

Thomas scolded, "That's wrong, Marcus!"

"I didn't mean any harm. I just wanted to get her attention. She's beautiful," winked Marcus.

"Get her attention?"

"Of course! She fell for it every time. And whenever I'd do it, she'd get upset. Poor Magdalene. And who'd be right there to comfort her? Me!"

Thomas shook his head in disgust.

"I'm sorry, Marcus," said Thomas, looking away sadly, "but that's wrong. You're anything but her hero."

Marcus glared at him, defensive now. "But my skills came in handy for you back there, didn't they?"

Marcus nodded back toward the gate. The auxiliary guards still had their swords drawn, nervously circling back to back, fending off their phantoms.

"Seems to me, you shouldn't be too quick to cast stones," Marcus smirked, wagging an accusing finger at Thomas.

NINE

THE BREEZE was offensively putrid. The garbage dump, established centuries before by King Josiah, reeked with its unending assortment of rubbish, exposed and rotting in the open air. Raw human waste, mixed with scraps of spoiled produce, littered countless acres below the Hinnom ridge. Entering the base of the ravine, Thomas and Marcus held their breaths as a light breeze fanned the stench in their direction.

"To think that pitiful beggars scavenge here," scoffed Marcus, noting a young urchin combing through the debris.

Darting out from a pile of refuse, a rat scurried across the path and over to where other vermin feasted on the decay and filth. Far ahead in the distance, a pack of wild street dogs, mangy with reddish hair and small tails, were savagely making rapid work of something they had found. Fierce canines, left to fend in the wild, were common around the Hinnom dump.

"There's no sign of Judas here. What would he ever be doing in a place like this?" Thomas asked.

"I saw it all," Marcus insisted. "Look. Right up there." He pointed upward and ahead. "He was in that tree on top of the ridge."

"He's not there now, Marcus. . ."

"I know what I saw!" Marcus insisted. "That's where he hung himself."

"Hung himself? I don't think so. Not Judas." Thomas sighed. "You dragged me out here for nothing, didn't you?"

"No, you just don't—"

"I don't want to hear it," Thomas replied testily. "I could still be sleeping right now."

"Will you at least listen to me?"

Irritated, Thomas sighed and nodded.

Marcus recounted what he had witnessed the day before. Walking nearby, he had happened to look up and spied a corpse dangling from the old redbud tree up above. Scaling the rocky side of the Hinnom for a closer look, Marcus discovered that it was Judas.

"Either he changed his mind while hanging from that tree," Thomas scoffed, "or you've got the wrong tree. Whichever, he's not there and we shouldn't be here!"

"Let's go a little further up," Marcus pleaded.

Walking the path of the dump was more difficult today than Marcus remembered it being the day before. In addition to contending with the usual heaps of refuse and waste, the path was now littered with loose rocks, soil and a boulder that had apparently slid down the ridge from the earthquake the afternoon before. The route was still passable; however, it was annoying having to choose between walking over loose rocks (and risking turning an ankle) or walking through the stench and mess of the city's debris.

Repulsed at the idea of walking through raw waste, Marcus didn't think twice about hiking over the rocks and dirt. Thomas, on the other hand, trudged straight through the garbage, as any fisherman would who wasn't averse to smelly messes. Over the rocks and around the debris, Marcus quickly met back up with Thomas.

There, both men stopped abruptly in the path.

Thomas recoiled, staggering clumsily backward onto the

rocks. Turning away, he tried to shake off the gruesome sight that he and Marcus had just stumbled upon.

"No," Thomas slowly moaned, fighting the urge to retch. He stammered, lips quivering, "It . . . can't be."

He squeezed his eyes shut, trying to erase the image from his mind.

"Oh, my God . . . Yahweh, no . . ."

Thomas buried his face in his hands.

"Haven't we had enough? This can't be. This was not supposed to happen!" His breathing was now ragged. He shook at the thought of what lay before him.

In contrast, Marcus stood quietly. Arms folded across his chest, chin set, eyes wide, he rocked nervously on his heels.

Suddenly, Thomas lunged forward, pushing Marcus aside.

"Go away, you mongrels!" he cursed at the small pack of wild dogs. The three ravenous animals looked up, snouts splattered crimson from their feast, barking, eyes fixed, incisors bared.

"Thomas, don't do it!" yelled Marcus.

But Thomas was deaf to all reasoning. Iron-jawed, his adrenaline surging, he seized a nearby tree branch, swinging it wildly at the dogs. Two of the mutts yelped and scampered away, turning back only to watch as the third dog caught the branch in his jaws and held on for the fight, snarling.

Oblivious to the danger, Thomas recoiled his foot and kicked hard at the beast. His toes, barely protected by the leather of his sandals, curled in pain as he kicked repeatedly at the dog's ribs. Finally, with a shrill yap, the dog relented and scurried away to join his two mangy friends.

Then Thomas fell to his knees—sobbing inconsolably before the grisly corpse that lay before him.

"Oh, Judas! Why?"

The body lay facedown in several inches of rainwater and sludge that had pooled from the showers a few days before. A frayed rope was tangled around its neck. It was tied off to a limb that had apparently splintered from a tree up above. The limb was scantly covered with a few green heart-shaped leaves that were partially scrunched and shredded. One remaining pea-shaped, purplish-pink flower on the redbud branch managed to survive the fall. The limb, under the strain of its load, had eventually splintered off during the earthquake, sending the body plummeting.

Turning Judas over, Thomas gasped and pulled the corpse toward his breast. As he cradled and rocked his friend, his chest convulsed as though his own heart was being torn to shreds on the Hinnom path.

WITH THE discovery of Judas' body, Marcus felt vindicated.

Of course I was right, he thought. *Maybe next time Thomas will be quicker to believe me!*

Curious, Marcus studied the tree. On the side of the trunk that faced the precipice was the splintered stub left by the broken limb. His contorted imagination replayed the snapping of the branch. Feet first, the swollen corpse would have plunged downward, hitting the craggy edge—tumbling, tangling, and crashing onto the rocky pavement below.

Death by hanging stretches the muscles, ligaments, and soft tissues of the neck. When Thomas turned Judas over, Marcus expected to see the neck roll limply to the side from being broken. Instead, it was stiffened from rigor—locked in an abnormal and contorted tilt.

With morbid fascination, Marcus observed that the skin tone was ashen. The victim's eyes were slightly open, crusty and scaly, and beginning to sink back into his skull. When he had worked the olive groves of his parents, Marcus had seen the decomposition of small rodents, but never of a human being.

While securely holding the body, Thomas cut the cord away from Judas' neck, gently freeing him from the ligature.

Running horizontally on the right side of the neck and upwards behind the left ear of the victim were the compression marks from the rope. Here a band of skin was cinched inward and appeared bruised. Sitting motionless, Thomas stared off into a distant place.

IT WAS only three years earlier that Thomas and Judas had first met. The two men were from entirely different backgrounds. The only thing either of them had in common was that they were not from the city. Thomas came from an area far north of Judea in Galilee. He was a fisherman with Peter and James. Judas was a rancher, tending his father's flocks in southern Judea, south of Hebron. Two men. Distant regions. Divergent occupations.

Although both of them were chosen by the Master to follow and learn, neither of them were part of the innermost circle. That was reserved for John, James, and Peter.

Thomas tried to be understanding when James and Peter (his fishing partners) were included in the inner circle but he wasn't. Of course it hurt a little.

"No," Thomas later admitted to Judas, "it actually hurt a lot."

What Thomas lacked in attention, he more than made up for in being the one to question and second-guess much of the disciples' activities. Often the Master would take Thomas aside and explain what was expedient and necessary, always with a smile and a parting wink, of course. To the pleasure of the other disciples, it came off as a scolding. Nonetheless, it was attention that Thomas craved, and that made him feel important.

Perhaps this was what had helped Thomas and Judas become the best of friends. Both were questioners. Judas, as the treasurer, had an accountant's disposition—obsessively tracking and balancing, checking and re-checking to make sure everything added up. Whenever the disciples blasted Thomas for his endless questions and doubts, he would just smile and give Judas a furtive nod as if to say, *Your turn!* Judas would then take up where Thomas had left off.

For Judas and Thomas, their comradeship became almost comical. Each fed off the other. Although the other disciples weren't amused, Thomas thought he once caught a faint chuckle from the Master. At any rate, they both got the attention they wanted by teaming up and becoming best of friends.

WHILE HOLDING his friend, Thomas recalled the pleasant memories of when he first invited Judas to go fishing. After passing through Samaria and before a time of ministry in Galilee, the Master had given them a day to relax and be refreshed, away from the crowds. Several of the disciples went fishing. Judas and Andrew paired up with Thomas in his boat.

"You'll have to teach me the tricks of the trade," remarked Judas. "You know, I've never done this before." Indeed, he had fished before, but only from the shore, never from a commercial vessel.

"It's easy, Judas," Thomas assured, saddling him with an extra heavy load of fishing nets and tackle.

As Judas approached the lakefront, it was apparent from his edginess that he was uneasy about the water. He much preferred land and made that perfectly clear from the outset.

With Thomas still on shore and Andrew in the boat, it was Judas' turn to get aboard. Clumsily, Judas put one foot in and then straddled the edge, trying to get his other foot in, jostling the boat from side to side. Trying to balance himself, but immobilized by fear, he just couldn't sit down.

From the back of the boat, Andrew quickly scrambled forward to calm Judas. He was a seasoned veteran when it came to boats and fishing, but he was anything but experienced when it came to assisting a panic-stricken passenger. In fright, Judas, all 215 pounds of him, grabbed onto Andrew, and together they keeled over into the shallow water. Both were completely soaked from head to toe, thrashing about. Laughing from the shore's gravel edge, just 10 feet away, Thomas laid back and roared uncontrollably until tears flowed.

NOW, JUST two short years later, Thomas lay on the gravelly pavement, sobbing uncontrollably, gently holding his friend's head out of the small pool of water.

This should never have happened. It doesn't even seem real, lamented Thomas. *Perhaps it's all just a bad dream. If I just doubt and second-guess it enough maybe it will all go away.*

But it wasn't going away.

Oh, Judas. You're my friend. Couldn't we have just gone fishing one more time? Couldn't we have shared just one more adventure?

By now the morning sun had crested well over the eastern horizon. The haze was clearing.

Next time, I'll board the boat first, bargained Thomas. *When you get in and feel off-balance or afraid, I'll steady you. I won't let anything happen to you. You won't fall over. Trust me. I'll be there for you. Just come back to me!*

The corpse still lay lifeless. No breath. No response.

The quills of remorse needled Thomas. *Why didn't I see this coming? How did I miss the signals? Somehow, you must have been feeling terribly afraid and desperate.*

Why wasn't I there for you? I could have helped you. I wouldn't have let anything happen to you.

As he sobbed, Thomas recalled the law and how abhorrent suicide was. Perhaps it was despicable not simply in view of its barbarity, but also because of the torment people endure in its wake.

"Friends don't let this happen to friends," Thomas wailed. "I'm so sorry, Judas. Please forgive me. I just didn't see it coming."

WHEN THOMAS shifted his stance and sat back, the victim's torso became visible. Marcus grimaced. It was sickening. His mind reeled and struggled to pull itself away from the carnage. But the grisly sight was now unshakably lodged in his brain.

Feeling chilled and queasy, Marcus staggered back and sat down. He then lurched sideways, coughing and gagging, his sides in spasms, retching. As he spit to clear his mouth and lay back to catch his breath, the light-headedness began to lift.

Although his stomach quickly emptied, his mind retained and replayed the gruesome sight of the spilled-out innards of Judas.

WHILE MARCUS' mind was on the mutilation, Thomas' thoughts lingered on the memories. Only six months earlier, Thomas had accompanied his friend on a trip south and was Judas' guest in his hometown of Kerioth.

Strangers were normally not welcomed by the Keriothians. What business would anyone have in coming to this frontier village? Citizens of this outpost were mostly poor, and anyone from the outside was suspected of being an agent of Rome, perhaps even a tax collector. Because Thomas came as the special guest and friend of their native son Judas, they treated him as warmly as they treated Judas, and even more so, with the hospitality that was traditionally extended to such friends.

It was there that Judas exposed Thomas to his world: the business of animal husbandry—the tending of sheep, goats, and cattle. Before long, Judas learned that Thomas was about as awkward in the Negeb fields as he, himself, was on the Sea of Galilee.

One time, Judas asked Thomas to drive some of the cattle toward a well. However, he conveniently forgot to instruct Thomas on the protocol for making the cattle move. On his own, Thomas decided to get behind one of the cows and push. Agitated and perturbed, the cow kicked backward and caught its hoof between Thomas' legs and up into his groin. As Thomas doubled over in pain, Judas ran to him to "rescue him." But as he neared Thomas, Judas doubled over himself—this time, with laughter.

Eventually Thomas caught his wind. Whimpering and groaning, he continued to feign injury. When he crawled close enough to where Judas stood, still laughing, he lunged for Judas' legs and tackled him to the ground. Together, Judas and Thomas, best of friends, wrestled each other to exhaustion. Then both lay on the ground and laughed. There, they affirmed their undying friendship, pledging to grow old together.

Now, just six months later, Thomas held his dear friend's corpse. *One more laugh,* he pleaded silently, *is that too much to ask?* Cradling Judas, he once again felt as though he'd been kicked unbearably hard. Only this time, the awful pain radiated throughout his soul.

STILL INSPECTING THE CORPSE, Marcus had further noticed that it was infested with insects and other vermin from the Hinnom dump. Rats, canines, and various insects had each paid their respects. Had Thomas not interceded, the wild dogs would have devoured their feast and scattered the bones.

Looking upward, Marcus envisioned that even before the branch had snapped and the body plummeted, flies would have already swarmed the corpse. From the moment of death, without the normal defenses a human being has, flesh flies had probably begun laying their eggs around the natural body openings of Judas' mouth, nose, and eyes.

With the body now splattered on the ground and the abdominal wall ruptured, the flies moved in with force, laying their eggs and producing the larva that thrive on decay. Even Marcus was repulsed at the thought of maggots moving throughout the corpse, spreading bacteria, secreting enzymes and, on the smallest levels, feeding on human tissue.

HOLDING HIS friend, Thomas fought to absorb the carnage before him. *How could this have happened? When did all this begin?*

Long before this day had ever come, on a level just as small—and as ravaging—as the maggots, Satan had wormed his way into Judas's life and begun feeding on the inner linings of his soul. The Teacher had often referred to Satan as Beelzebub, meaning "the lord of the flies." Quietly and undetected, unseen but very real, darkness had entered in—secreting its seed that later hatched and swarmed—gnawing inwardly on Judas' mind and will.

"Judas, why did you leave me?" cried Thomas.

Pity now turned to anger.

"You are cursed. Do you hear me? Cursed!"

Still holding the tangled rope and splintered branch, Thomas abruptly pushed the corpse aside and stood up. Shaking the cord at his friend, hand quivering, he scowled, "You've forsaken me, you wretch. How could you do this?"

Thomas finally realized that, while he and Judas had been the best of friends, and alike in so many ways, they had still been very different.

All along, while Thomas had been a doubter about everything but himself, Judas had been confident in everything but himself. While it seemed that Thomas had questioned everything, Judas had questioned only himself. When Thomas had taken forever to believe the impossible, Judas found it only impossible to believe in himself. These differences distinguished the two men, and had now caused their vow of undying friendship to be severed.

Trembling in confusion and anger, Thomas lingered among the debris and garbage. The canines kept a steady watch from a distance. Marcus was waiting, sitting back on the loose debris from the landslide, taking aim at nearby rats with a handful of stones.

Today, when so many new questions had been raised—first with the loss of his Master and now with the loss of his best friend, Thomas wasn't sure if there was anything worth believing in. Holding the strand of frayed rope, twisting it around and off the branch, he turned and trudged away from the dump, walking listlessly back toward Jerusalem.

Marcus was forgotten, left behind to menace the rats. Hopefully, he would stay put and guard the corpse. Someone had to go tell the Iscariots what had happened.

TEN

SOMBERLY, Ruhamah studied the brass ring she clutched while standing alongside the road. Surrounding her were Martha, Miriam, Elisheba, and other women who wailed in traditional anticipation of the funeral bier. The ring's once polished surface was now dull and nicked from the passing of time. The previously circular thin band was now oblong and bent from wear.

Turning the ring over in her palm evoked memories of when she used to tickle and massage the toes of her baby boy. His newborn skin was perfectly soft and fresh. As she cradled him, Ruhamah would smile and blow small kisses. Baby Judas, in turn, cooed and giggled back at her. In moments like this, a new mother could only wish that her infant would stay eternally innocent, and she would always be able to protect him from injury.

Thirteen years later, as her pride and joy entered manhood, her husband bartered a mere 27 copper coins for this brass ring. They were poor and did the best they could. A gold or silver band was out of the question.

Today, with her firstborn now dead, to suggest that this simple ornament was cheap or worthless would be an affront to a mother's love. Although the ring was only common brass, it was still priceless.

The temple guards had taken her son. They dare not take anything else from her. She would give this ring and a thousand others just to have her son back, to hold him in her arms. By kneading the ring, warming it in her hands, she comforted herself with the illusion that none of this was real—defying the report that had sent her reeling earlier that day.

AS RUHAMAH awoke that morning, there was the ring, Judas' ring, resting on the table near their bed. Picking up the small, thin band and inspecting it, Ruhamah turned to her husband and asked, "Simeon, what do you know about this?"

"That belongs to Judas."

"I know that. But why is it lying here?"

"How should I know? Ask your son," replied Simeon, rubbing his eyes and shaking his head, trying to awaken.

"It just seems unusual," Ruhamah said.

"Perhaps he left it from last night. Forgot to put it on this morning."

"I don't know if he even came home last night. He wasn't in by the time we went to bed."

"He probably had some work to do this morning. Didn't want to dirty it up."

"But it's not like Judas to take his ring off. And why would he put it beside our bed?" Ruhamah grew increasingly concerned and clutched the ring to her breast fearfully.

Seeing his wife's apprehension triggered an uneasy feeling in Simeon as well. It occurred to him that temple guards might be hunting down the followers of the Teacher. *What if they seized Judas?*

Ah, but the boy is smart, he thought. Simeon felt confident that Judas knew how to take care of himself. If anything, Judas left the ring so that if the temple guards ever found him, he would not be carrying identification. Then he wouldn't be so easily linked to the disciples. *He'll be all right!*

AS THE women waited in the afternoon sun, nothing was all

right. In the middle of the women stood Ruhamah, swaddled in her shroud of mourning. The coarse garment was sackcloth, made of black goat's hair. Sackcloth was a thick mesh used primarily for grain sacks, but also for bedding livestock. It was the clothing of paupers. This raiment of mourning signaled her utter abasement and poverty of spirit.

From a distance, Ruhamah could see the dispirited processional now slowly moving in their direction. Squinting through her tears, she saw that it was John, Andrew, James, and Thomas who carried the bier.

"Dear Thomas," she whispered, "you were always there—like a son to me."

EARLIER THAT morning, Ruhamah helped Elisheba with the breakfast cleanup. For the last five years, Tubal and Elisheba enjoyed hosting the Iscariots in their home during the Passover. Each year, the dark, narrow, arched streets of Jerusalem swarmed with its citizens and pilgrims. Tubal and Simeon were second cousins, so the Iscariots knew that they always had a place to lodge during the annual festivities.

During the Passover week, all leaven was carefully purged from one's diet. Because the food eaten that week was different, every morsel was a reminder to the children that the season was a special one. The breakfast that Elisheba served that morning consisted of fire-roasted wheat kernels prepared the day before, three kinds of cheese, sweet syrup made from boiled grapes, and date cakes—unleavened, of course.

Suddenly, a loud rapping on the front door broke their morning leisure.

"Ignore it," Tubal said to his guests. "It's just the lad from down the street bartering his eggs."

The rapping continued, harder now.

Tubal yelled toward the door, "Go away! It's the Sabbath. We can't—"

The door crashed open. Thomas stood there, breathing heavily, eyes reddened and hands trembling.

He quickly slammed the door behind him.

"What on earth has gotten into you?" Elisheba reproved. "It's barely the third hour of the day!"

Tubal, perceiving the alarm in Thomas' eyes, pulled up a stool. He motioned for him to sit.

"No, I can't sit. You—" Thomas pointed to Ruhamah and Simeon, "need to sit."

At this, Ruhamah walked slowly over to Thomas, her body trembling.

"What is it, Thomas? What's the matter?"

"Please, Ruhamah. Sit down," Thomas insisted, glancing over at Simeon for help.

Simeon stepped in from behind, steadied his wife and guided her back to the stool.

Thomas stood by the table, struggling to collect himself. His chest was tight, his breathing ragged. His eyes deliberately shifted away, afraid of looking directly at either Simeon or Ruhamah.

Glancing toward Tubal, Thomas searched for the right words.

"Judas . . ." Thomas muttered, struggling for composure. His voice wavered. "Judas, he's . . . gone."

"What?" Simeon was in disbelief. "What do you mean, 'he's gone'?"

"It's . . . he . . . he's just gone," Thomas faltered, shrinking back from the painful truth.

"Where has Judas gone?" demanded Ruhamah.

Simeon and Ruhamah knew that most of the disciples were in hiding, perhaps in the house of Miriam. However, the whereabouts of Peter were still unknown and rumors were already circulating about his safety. Simeon and Ruhamah had supposed that Judas was in seclusion with the remaining disciples.

"You don't understand," pleaded Thomas, looking Ruhamah directly in the eyes.

Thomas wished there was some other way to tell her. He wished there was something other than this to tell her. He didn't want to hurt her. It would cut her deeply. What do you say to a mother?

"Your son is . . . " Thomas choked. He couldn't do it.

Simeon finished the pronouncement himself. ". . . dead?"

The room was suspended in an icy hush.

Thomas nodded slowly.

Staring at the disciple, Ruhamah slowly shook her head. *Unthinkable! Impossible!* Her soul balked at the incredulity of such a report. *How could Thomas say such a hurtful thing?*

"That can't be true. It's not true!" she cried.

Ruhamah trembled in denial, mouth gaping and eyes ablaze. "Thomas, tell me you're wrong! Not my boy. Not Judas. He's my son. He's all right. Tell me he's all right!"

But as Ruhamah pleaded with Thomas, he kept his eyes fixed on hers, refusing to let her go, refusing to abandon her in this horrific moment of shock. Slowly, he nodded again.

"Cursed are you, Thomas!" cried Ruhamah. "You're a lying messenger. Tell me it's not true. Tell me!"

Then she turned to Tubal. "He's mistaken. He's lying!"

Tubal looked away, stunned, trying to repel the darkness that now eclipsed their morning.

Ruhamah protested, "No, Thomas!"

"I'm so sorry." Thomas reached toward her.

Convulsing with sobs, Ruhamah staggered from her chair and sank to the floor.

Elisheba huddled next to her, struggling to be strong, holding her friend. She pulled Ruhamah's dark hair back from her face, combing her fingers gently through it, sharing her sorrow.

Pacing furiously, Simeon went into the adjoining room. Tubal backed away, giving his cousin time alone.

From the next room, Tubal, Elisheba and Ruhamah could hear the sounds of ripping fabric. In the Jewish tradition, the first duty of the grieving was to rend their clothes, tearing one or more of their inner garments. The tear was generally about a handbreadth in length.

In Simeon's case, this shredded garment would never be repaired. *Do You see what You've done, God? Do You see my heart?* he cried. In most cases, a garment is mended after the thirteenth day of mourning. However, in the tradition of grieving parents, this rip would never be closed again. For Simeon, the torn garment was more than just a precept of the law; it signaled the tearing and tattering of his heart.

Numb and confused, Simeon re-entered the room and asked Thomas, "Who got to him? The soldiers? The temple guards?"

His tone became angry, cold. "They've done to Judas what they did to that Teacher, haven't they?"

Thomas was now even more reluctant to explain.

"No. . ." He paused, searching for the words. "That's not what happened."

"Then what?" pressed Simeon.

Thomas pulled Simeon back into the adjoining room, nodding for Tubal to follow them. There, in hushed conversation away from the women, he detailed where he and Marcus had found Judas and what they had seen.

Horrified, but struggling to remain calm, Simeon quizzed Thomas further. "What was in Judas' mind? What would make him do this?"

Inwardly, Simeon reasoned with himself, *My son was not a bad man!*

But still, he questioned Thomas, "Why would he kill himself? With the execution of the Teacher and everyone so upset,

117

why didn't Judas just go hide with the rest of the disciples? In their company, he could have at least found encouragement. Why did he kill himself?"

It was a tragic puzzle, void of both solutions and consolation. Thomas had no answers for Simeon, at least not yet. The only thing Thomas could tell him was where Judas lay fallen.

ELEVEN

CLOSER, BUT ever so slowly, the funeral procession plodded, now just a short distance away. Simeon had sent strict orders that his wife and the other women were not to follow them to where Judas had been found. They must wait alongside the road southeast of Jerusalem in the Valley of Hinnom, just before it branches off toward the Kidron Valley.

Laboring under the physical and mental load of their burden, the four disciples carried their fallen comrade. Andrew and James took the lead, with John and Thomas in back, each with a pole on their shoulders, the bier raised high.

Closed coffins were unknown to the grieving band. The closest thing to a coffin was the sarcophagus, like that which once held the body of Joseph in Egypt. Instead, a bier or stretcher was used to transport the dead. The pole at each corner made it easier for mourners to carry the corpse.

As Ruhamah watched the procession inch closer, something about this burial process seemed indecently wrong. She had been to many funerals before. Burial of the dead usually took place, if possible, within 24 hours after death, and even frequently on the very day of death. Before today, that timetable had always seemed quite reasonable.

But today her heart protested against the time restraints imposed by the law. *Can't they get here more quickly?* she fumed. *I want to see my son. Don't they realize that this is not just any son? This is my son.* The granules of time were quickly slipping away and the men were trudging ever so slowly.

I want to see my son now!

Conversely, her heart feuded, *Why did a burial have to be so hurried in the first place? Who made up such unsympathetic laws? Who's in such a hurry to bid my son farewell?*

Indeed, the law urged this haste. The rapidity of decomposition, the volatility of grief, and the reluctance to allow the dead to remain long in the houses of the living for fear of defilement and judgment were all reasons behind this urgency. Even so, with a handful of mourners, a typical procession would occasionally halt while short addresses were delivered.

Today, however, there was no halting. There were no funeral orations. For Ruhamah, everything was happening too fast. Just this morning she had learned of her son's death. Now, a mere five hours later, she was pressed to bid him farewell.

To add insult to injury, Elisheba reminded her that this was the Sabbath and that the chief mourning rites were to be postponed until after the Sabbath. Although Ruhamah didn't argue, and Elisheba didn't press the issue, it still hurt that this restriction was even mentioned.

How insensitive! I have to bury my feelings just to keep everyone else happy on the Sabbath? Praise Yahweh God that at least I'm allowed to do what is needful to bury my son. At least I'm allowed to walk beyond the Sabbath limits to lay him to rest. Praise Yahweh God that my son was not a slave. God be with those mothers! The codes of the rabbis didn't even allow those mothers to mourn publicly—ever!

What also seemed odd about this processional was that her son's mourners were so few in number. *It's because the other disciples are still in seclusion,* she reasoned. Perhaps the temple guards are also watching. She wouldn't put it past the temple guards to have menaced the few family and friends that had gathered.

Others who waited with Ruhamah privately considered that the meager attendance might be related to the notion that a premature death signified the disfavor of God. Indeed, Judas had died too young. Death before 50 years of age signaled the presence of evil and the requisite punishment. This one was young, cut off from Israel like premature fruit that falls from the vine. To die at 60 years of age was regarded as death at the hands of heaven. At 70, it was regarded as that of an old man.

The more Ruhamah thought of these things, the more cynical she became. Perhaps if we just had a few shekels to throw around. Would that help? Would a little silver do? Or even some gold staters?

Those who had enough money would typically hire professional mourners to accompany the funeral. They would wail, letting others know of the death as they passed through the city streets. Traditionally in Judea, the hired mourners preceded the bier. In Galilee, they followed behind. If Ruhamah and Simeon had the means to hire such mourners, as obnoxious as they were, it would have at least boosted the attendance at this procession, padding its dignity. But they had no money and so the mourners were scarce.

Finally, the procession arrived at where the women were waiting. Without breaking stride, John and James kept their eyes focused ahead. Andrew and Thomas glanced over toward the women. Slowing his pace, Thomas steadied his gaze at Ruhamah.

"Be strong, my sons," Simeon urged. "Keep moving!"

As the bier whisked by, the women could almost see the form of Judas beneath the disheveled burial sheets. It was obvious that the body had been prepared and loaded onto the bier without the care and attention of a woman's touch.

But the men had done their best, considering what they'd

found. When Simeon, Thomas, and a few of the disciples arrived where Marcus was waiting, they made quick preparation of Judas' body.

Methodically, Simeon had begun by closing his son's eyes. This act signified that death was acknowledged by the closest of kin. It further signified that the one who died was now released to depart into the afterlife.

Simeon then closed his son's mouth and bound up his jaw. Never again would he hear his son's voice. Oh, just to talk with him one last time. Simeon's tears fell on the swollen face of Judas. Just to have the chance to say goodbye.

As the bier approached the waiting women, Tubal could see his wife wagging her head disapprovingly at their shabby burial preparations. She, nor any of the other women, would ever be told of the gruesome scene where Judas was found, or the mess they'd had to deal with. This corpse could not have been handled with the level of tidiness that was otherwise customary.

Typically, a body was brought to a home for careful washing and preparation before burial. It was traditional to anoint the body with aromatic ointments. Clean clothes that were normally worn in life would replace the old clothes. Feet and hands would be swathed with grave bands. The face would then be covered or bound about with a napkin or handkerchief. Finally, a sheet would be neatly stretched over the bier in preparation for the trek to the grave.

The law prescribed that during this time, all necessary food was to be prepared outside the house, and if possible, not to be eaten in the presence of the dead. As long as the corpse was actually in the house, one was forbidden to eat meat, drink wine, wear the ritual prayer bands, or even engage in study.

The body of Judas, however, was in no condition to be brought back inside the city walls or into a house to be cleaned up and prepared for burial.

"Halt the procession!" ordered Ruhamah. "Now!"

She broke free of the women and ran to the front of the bier, pushing against James and Andrew to stop them and pulling at the bier.

"You will let me see my son!"

Seeing the bier totter, the other women gasped, fearing the corpse might just topple off.

Tubal cast a look of irritation at Elisheba for not restraining her. He then scurried around to the front and held Ruhamah.

"Uncover him!" demanded Ruhamah.

Instinctively the disciples lowered the bier. The women struggled to restrain Ruhamah.

"Let me see my son!" she demanded.

Everyone, except Ruhamah, had been told the nature of Judas' death. They were aware that the death was self-inflicted. Between the plunge down the cliff, the length of decomposition, and the ravaging from the pests and dogs, the corpse was in no shape to be viewed. Under no circumstances was Ruhamah to be permitted to see it.

"Why are you doing this to me?" she cried. "The guards have taken my son's life. Would you now rob me of my last chance to see him?"

Had Tubal not again warned his wife with an unspoken wag of his head, she would have suggested that they at least allow this mother to see her son's face. However, the corpse dared not be viewed. Even beneath the covering, it was apparent that the head was contorted sideways. Dangling partially out from beneath the covering was a blackened hand, darkened by the pooling of blood.

"No!" said Simeon gruffly.

Then stepping closer to Ruhamah, who was recoiling in disbelief, he put his arm around her and held her. For the first time in this horrible day, Simeon embraced his grieving wife—

123

PRISON BOOK PROJECT
P.O. Box 1146
Sharpes, FL 32959

breaking from his own anger and sorrow, just for a moment, to give her the husbandly support and compassion she needed.

"I'm sorry, my dear," Simeon offered tenderly through his own tears. "Please, you must trust me. Let your last memory of our son, alive and happy, be the image you forever carry in your heart."

Ruhamah then steadied her gaze at Miriam. Her next words were unnerving.

"I will see my son again, in paradise—that's what the Teacher told us. Is this right?"

Miriam was speechless.

Ruhamah waited, her eyes locked on Miriam's.

"Answer me. It's true, isn't it? I will see him!" she pressed.

Miriam knew that Ruhamah was not aware that her son's death was by self-murder. Her question was only about the hope of paradise. *Help me,* Miriam prayed, searching for the right answer—an answer that would comfort a grieving mother and be compatible with the circumstances of suicide.

According to the Hebrew code, no special law is found against this crime, although it is included in the prohibition against killing. Nevertheless, because of the high value the Hebrews placed on human life, suicide was viewed with deep abhorrence. Only the most degraded and despairing would ever take his own life.

As evil and repugnant as self-murder was, Miriam also re-called how the Master would teach that all sins could be forgiven. *However, must not one first want forgiveness?* she pondered. *To be forgiven, must not someone really want it?* That much seemed clear to her. Absolution must be desired and sought after.

And if a man hangs himself, would there even be a moment of conscious sanity for him to change his mind, to truly repent and cry out to God—even if his deed could not be reversed? Would God—could God—forgive such selfishness and evil?

124

Her mind seesawed with the possibilities and implications. Then again, to suppose that God could forgive self-murder, wouldn't that incite the next desperate soul?

Then it came to her.

Miriam held Ruhamah's hand. Looking intently into her puffy eyes, she smiled gently and spoke softly.

"God is a just God," Miriam offered. Her words were measured, yet assuring. "Merciful is He. The Master has told us that He is not willing that any should perish."

With that, Ruhamah dropped her gaze and settled back in her spirit. Her question was answered, at least for now.

Quickly the bier was again lifted onto the shoulders of the disciples. Together, the mourners continued the dolorous march.

AS SHE followed along, Ruhamah recalled another funeral.

Judas had once enthusiastically told her of a time when Jesus interrupted a funeral at the village of Nain. Nain was located about four miles from Tabor and 25 miles southwest of Capernaum. It sat on the northwestern slope of a hill called "Little Hermon."

Just outside the city gates of Nain, the Lord met up with this funeral procession. First came the women. Among them was the widowed mother, whose only treasure was to be hidden from her forever. Judas had remarked that her sorrow caught the attention of the Lord. Right there in the roadway, He halted the procession, touched the bier, and suddenly the boy awakened—alive!

If only the temple guards had not executed the Teacher, she considered. *If only Jesus was here. If only Judas' death had happened just a week earlier. If only . . .*

Ruhamah then lashed out at God. *You could have stopped this,* she seethed. *This madness could have been interrupted. This nightmare could have ended by now. But no, my son is still dead!*

WHILE RUHAMAH was chaffering for a miracle, Simeon thought back on his unexpected visit from the priests a few hours earlier. Thomas and Simeon had left the house of Tubal and headed south toward the city gate, to the Hinnom Valley to find Judas. Unexpectedly, they were met on the way by some of the religious leaders and temple guards.

Seeing the guards, Thomas tensed up and readied himself for a confrontation. However, the priests stepped ahead of the guards, their hands open, extending a show of sympathy.

"Rumor has come to us about your son's untimely death," the lead priest consoled. "May we be thy expiation!"

It was well known that under exceptional circumstances, priests were allowed to mourn for the dead. However, something about their mannerisms seemed odd.

"Be ye blessed of heaven," Simeon politely replied, as was a customary response when a priest mourned for one's deceased.

"We know that your son followed the Teacher. Poor, misdirected boy," they moaned. "His anguish was just too great."

Although Simeon wasn't aware of the priests' involvement in Jesus' execution, Thomas was fully aware of their corruption and did everything to restrain himself. They were snakes, but this was no time for belligerence. Simeon needed to get to his son.

"We know you are from out of town and are of pitiful means," the priest continued. "A field has recently been purchased where foreigners, transients, and the poor can be laid to rest. It is the old brick maker's field—the potter's field."

"A brick maker's field?" Simeon asked.

The priest explained that it was a field formerly used to dig clay for making pottery and bricks. For years now, the field had been abandoned and was unfit for tillage.

"The old brick maker's price eventually dropped to 30 pieces of silver," the priest gloated and chuckled—jabbing Thomas. "Barely the cost of a slave, wouldn't you say?"

"Since it's just wasteland," he continued, "and good for only a cemetery, we'll use it for charity funerals. You can bury your son there."

As the priests departed, something deep within Thomas protested. Those foul buffoons. Something's just too suspicious.

Nevertheless, Thomas kept his mouth shut. He knew that Simeon and Ruhamah didn't have the money for a proper burial. How could they refuse such a deal?

THE PROCESSION branched off on the road that led away from the Hinnom ravine and headed southeast toward the Kidron valley. Just at the far eastern edge of the Hinnom was a narrow plateau, a level plot, more than halfway up the hillside. Located here was the old brick maker's field. It measured approximately 78 by 57 feet. The soil on the hill was chalky.

Arriving ahead of the procession to dig the grave were Thaddaeus and Matthew. Because Thaddaeus was so strong, he did most of the digging while Matthew supervised. The one time Thaddaeus took a break and passed the shovel, Matthew just pecked at the hole, complaining about everything that had gone wrong the last 24 hours. When the procession was in sight, Thaddaeus grabbed the shovel from Matthew and hustled to finished the grave himself, admonishing Matthew to stop his whining.

SLOWLY, THE mourners ascended the hillside. Halfway up, the disciples lowered the bier from their shoulders to their waists, in order to reposition their load. Ruhamah could now again see her son's form, swaddled by the grave sheet.

Traditionally, mothers carried their infants to burial. Children over 12 months were transported on a bed or stretcher, like an adult. As they neared the grave, Ruhamah's Nain miracle was not to be. *Just let me hold him one last time.*

Let me carry my baby, she prayed. She had carried him to his cradle as a baby—why couldn't she now carry him to his grave? Simeon kept a firm grip on his wife, steadying her in the climb and restraining her from lunging at the bier.

At the crest of the plateau, the bier was laid next to the shallow grave. Standing on the chalky soil next to this final resting place, all were silent.

In keeping with tradition, mourners were not to be tormented by the needless talk of others. All were supposed to observe silence until addressed by them.

In most funerals, a priest would begin by asking, "Inquire for the ground of mourning." If a rabbi was present, he would reply, "God is a just judge," which meant that He had removed a near relative. Then an elaborate oration of comfort was read, followed by scripted expressions of consolation.

However, today no priests or rabbis were present. To the relief of Ruhamah, no synagogue officials showed up to recite cold prayers of pity. As it was, everything about this funeral procession had already been too cursory, too cold and formulated, and too protective of her emotions.

The friends and family that had gathered were finally settled for a few moments of true compassion and unscripted reflection. One at a time, each offered tender words of encouragement. Remarks of comfort emanated from true feelings, not stale formulas. In that little plateau cemetery, in a field previously abandoned and unfit for tillage, loving-kindness was bountifully sowed.

As the bier was lowered into the grave, Thomas shut his eyes and breathed deeply, too tired to cry anymore, but still unwilling to release his friend. After just three years of companionship, two men—both unique in their insecurities, but united in comradeship—would part ways forever.

IMMEDIATELY AFTER the final heaps of dirt were placed,

Thomas planned to depart for the safety of Galilee. He would withdraw from anything or anyone that demanded faith or hope. For at least a week, he would go back to fishing. There, he would reminisce and search for sure footing amidst the grief that had left him feeling so unsteady and unsure.

During the final graveside prayer, Thomas felt a gentle nudge against his left hand. Determined to ignore the intrusion, he kept his eyes tightly shut—unmoved and aloof.

Two hands then wrapped around his hand. One traced the outside of his fingers; the other pried them open. A small object was placed into his palm, then both hands closed tightly about his hand. Cupped securely in his fist, still radiating the warmth of a mother's devotion, was the thin band of brass.

TWELVE

RETURNING TO MIRIAM'S house, the mourners of Judas were greeted by a bountiful spread of food generously prepared by neighboring friends. The meal consisted of bread, hard-boiled eggs, lentils, and an abundance of fish from the lake of Gennesaret—all served on the finest of earthenware.

During the middle course of the meal, when most everyone had settled down and began to unwind, two visitors came knocking on Miriam's door. It was Nicodemus and Yoseph of Arimathea.

"Haven't we had enough?" Miriam said. "What do you two want now?"

"Miriam, we need to talk."

"It's the Sabbath. Is there no rest? This is a day of mourning. Leave us be."

"Please, Miriam," Yoseph said softly, trying to calm her.

"It's important," said Nicodemus, pulling a linen night-shirt from his satchel bag.

Yoseph took it and held it up. "This belongs to someone here," he said. "We think it belongs to Marcus."

Miriam snatched it from Yoseph.

"Why do you have it?" asked Miriam. "What makes you think it belongs to my son?"

Nicodemus explained that he had seen it earlier that morning at the dwelling of the Sanhedrin high command.

When he asked about it, Nicodemus was told of the events of the night before, during which Marcus and Thomas were detained.

Nicodemus continued, "They grabbed this off someone who was spotted in the Gethsemane garden at the very same time the Teacher was arrested. Miriam, your son—he may be headed for trouble. He shouldn't have been there."

At this, Miriam turned and quickly called for her son.

Marcus appeared in the doorway. "What do you want?"

"Is this yours?" quizzed Miriam, holding out the nightshirt.

He glanced at the shirt and then looked away. Marcus shrugged his shoulders.

"Marcus?"

"I don't know!" he said angrily.

Miriam pressed, "Marcus, this was taken from someone in the garden of Gethsemane two nights ago. You told me you were with friends that night."

"I was out!" Marcus said, defensively.

"Tell me this fits one of the other disciples, Marcus," she said as she held it up to his chest. "Go ahead. Which one does this belong to?"

Marcus was silent.

"This is yours, isn't it?" Miriam pressed.

Marcus finally lashed out, "So what if it is?"

"Then you were there!" Miriam was flushed with anger and fear. "Don't you know that you could've been arrested? Or worse, killed?"

"Come on, Mother. I'm not a child."

"Of course you're not. You're 21," she cried. "But yesterday we lost the Teacher, and today it was Judas. We still don't know where Peter is. Will you be next?"

Marcus frowned at her, unsure what to say.

Miriam continued, "You have a knack for not being where

you should be and for being where you shouldn't be. If you want to be treated like a man, you need to start acting like one!"

At this, Marcus exploded. "If it wasn't for me, Mother, Judas would still be rotting beside the roadway!"

Miriam was aghast.

From the other room, the guests who had been eavesdropping now only heard deafening silence—followed by a loud SMACK!

Touching his cheek, Marcus stared at his mother in disbelief.

Miriam sank her face in her hands and began to cry softly.

From behind Miriam, Thaddaeus stepped forward. "What do you mean, Marcus, 'If it wasn't for me'?"

Marcus looked away, defiant.

But Thaddaeus grabbed him by the shoulders, "Talk to me, Marcus. How did you know where Judas was?"

"I, uh . . . I saw it all!" Marcus spilled it out. "That's right. I saw everything!"

In the doorway, Nicodemus and Yoseph stared at him, dumbstruck. Thaddaeus kept a grip on Marcus' shoulder. "Tell us the truth now. What did you see?"

At this, Marcus began to tremble. Eyes turning red and tearing, he shrugged off Thaddaeus and turned to Miriam. "Judas cheated you, Mother!"

"What?" Miriam gasped.

"I said 'the truth,' Marcus!" Thaddaeus warned.

Miriam waved Thaddaeus off.

"Mother, he cheated you. I told you not to trust him. The money you gave for the treasury, he—"

"No, Marcus!" Miriam interrupted.

"Let me finish. Father worked hard for that money. It was ours. It was mine!" Marcus cried. "And Judas—he took it all. And you, Mother—you just gave it all away. You just threw it to the wind. You've acted so strange since father died. I know it's been difficult, but still, people have taken advantage of you!"

At that, Miriam pulled her son close to her. Although he was now a man, he was still her little boy. And today, her boy was hurting. Years of pent-up anguish were now spilling out. His frustration was honest. His father was sorely missed. The ache was still so real. Only in the care of the Teacher had she found solace and a reason to live. Marcus had yet to share in that peace.

The gifts she had given for the Teacher's work were for Him alone, not for Judas, nor even for the other disciples. If Judas or anyone else had squandered the gifts, such matters were out of her hands and between them and God.

As she held Marcus in a tight embrace, she whispered through her tears, "It's all right, Marcus. There's plenty for all. There's still plenty for you, too. God has blessed us. The Teacher has told us that where our treasure is, there our hearts will be, also."

Only a mother can best read her son. As Marcus wept in her arms, she sensed that something within him was still unsettled. "What is it, Marcus? There's something more, isn't there?"

Collecting himself, Marcus said, "Do you want to know why Judas hung himself?"

For a few moments, Thaddaeus, Nicodemus, and Yoseph had looked away and given Miriam and her son some privacy. But now their attention was again riveted on Marcus.

"When no one was looking," Marcus revealed, "Judas struck a bargain."

Miriam shook her head in disbelief.

"It was two nights ago," he continued. "It was with the religious leaders. I know what I saw. When Judas left the Passover meal, I snuck out and followed him."

Thaddaeus began to speak up, but Miriam waved him off again, gently urging Marcus on. "And what did you see? It's all right, my son, you can tell us."

"For the price of a slave, just 30 measly shekels of silver, Judas betrayed the Teacher!"

"That can't be," protested Thaddaeus.

Marcus persisted, "Think about it! Where did the religious leaders suddenly come up with the money for the old brick maker's field? Why do you think they offered the first burial plot to the parents of Judas—just a coincidence? Or to soothe their consciences?"

Thaddaeus scratched his head, absorbing what he was hearing, piecing it together.

"Don't you remember?" Marcus continued. "At Gethsemane, near the stone press, before the temple guards ever arrived, Judas came in. The guards must have been hiding in the distant trees. Remember the greeting? The kiss—it was a signal."

Thaddaeus nodded slowly, accepting it.

"It was a set-up, and the Teacher knew it," Marcus continued. "That's when the arrest happened. Yes, I was there in the garden. I admit it!"

"Marcus, look at me." Miriam was again seeing something in her son's eyes that only a mother could see.

"Is there anywhere else you've been? Is there anything else you're hiding from us that we need to know?" she pressed.

Marcus squirmed.

"Tell us now, and you won't get in trouble," she promised.

Marcus' lips quivered. He looked down.

"Talk to me," his mother entreated. "Please!"

Marcus hesitated. Then he looked back at her. "There is something."

THIRTEEN

TO THE east of Jerusalem, across the Kidron valley, the great temple flung its late afternoon shadow upon the small hillside olive grove. Hurriedly, the hired farmer dragged his large willow basket across the olive yard and into the grove's center where his mangy old mule waited patiently.

Usually, Theudas worked much slower, but the violent earth tremor and subsequent aftershocks had damaged some of the oldest trees. Theudas was in a race against time to salvage the olive berries that had fallen. Although it was the Sabbath, this work couldn't wait. Hopefully, the landowner wouldn't discover that he was working and enforce the mandated rest.

When Tobijah was still alive to run the land, the Sabbath was rarely regarded; however, since Tobijah's death, his widow—Miriam of Jerusalem—seemed increasingly partial to the rest day. Nevertheless, today there was risk to the harvest. The crop needed attention.

Earlier in the day, a stray passerby had asked about the age of the grove's tallest gnarly trees. Theudas impatiently shrugged his shoulders and brushed him aside.

Usually, Theudas wouldn't have been so rude, but today's hurried pace had left him feeling as old and contorted as some of the trees themselves. He wasn't just a common hireling, employed for a limited time. For 17 years he'd worked this orchard; and today, he felt the weight of all those years as he stooped to pick up the berries. Today, he was in no mood for idle chitchat.

As much as he grumbled inside, old Theudas really did take pride in this work. The cultivation of olive trees and the harvest of their berries was an honorable work that went back to the earliest times in Canaan. The olive tree was the "king" of trees in this region, serving a vital role in the economy.

Many olive trees grew wild on bare and rocky ground, but Miriam's grove was situated on a nicely terraced hillside just east of the great city. Its thin soil layer rested only a few sandy inches above a hard limestone ledge. The long, dry summers afforded the perfect conditions for the trees to yield their fruit.

Four years ago, before Tobijah died, the grove was considered off-limits to any visitors, allowing Theudas to work undistracted. Two years after Tobijah's death, however, Miriam had Theudas take down a portion of the three-foot stone wall so that any person who wished could enter the orchard.

To Theudas' chagrin, now anyone could pilfer olive berries from the trees. Women and girls would pick mature berries from the lowest of branches, while the young men climbed higher, often daring one another to reach the highest of boughs. Their reckless adventures sometimes left branches stripped, bent and even broken. Other boys just came for the mischief—deliberately picking the hard, unripe berries to throw at each other.

What a mess, thought Theudas. *Doesn't Miriam realize that her strange ways are costing her money?* More than once, Miriam had explained to Theudas that she wanted the small plantation to serve as a public resting place from the hot afternoon sun. *And she calls this her "mission"?* Theudas spat.

Theudas was further disgruntled by the fact that Miriam enforced the Deuteronomy law regarding gleaning. Although the yield of an olive crop was unpredictable from year to year, Miriam insisted that after the olives were beat from the trees,

Theudas was not to go over the branches a second time. The remains were to be left for the stranger, the fatherless, and the widowed. She insisted that this applied not just to the locals, but to the poor from neighboring communities as well. That being the rule, Theudas was even more thorough the first time he harvested the berries from the branches.

Beat 'em hard before they come a beatin'! Theudas chuckled to himself.

Eventually the inquisitive man wandered away and Theudas returned to his work. After another hour, Theudas emerged from the trees dragging a large basket of just-picked olives. He again tensed up, this time at the sight of another loiterer. It was a lone figure walking slowly around the oil press.

The rock-cut oil press was where Theudas milled the olive berries—cracking and crushing them, pressing and squeezing them, until the beaten oil seeped out from the berries. Other farmers, who could afford the eight drachmas that Theudas charged, would bring their harvest to the grove to be processed. Those who couldn't afford it simply crushed their olive berries the old-fashioned way—tramping out the oil by foot. This new intruder, however, carried no olives to be milled.

What is it now? sighed Theudas impatiently.

The man appeared homeless—clothes dirty, hair disheveled, his face bearing the marks of suffering and deprivation. He seemed paranoid and agitated. His hands quivered as they surveyed the surface of the oil press, feeling the irregularity of its hard texture.

"Move aside!" snapped Theudas. The late afternoon sun accentuated every wrinkle on his tired, weather-beaten face.

"I'm sorry, sir. I just came to —"

"To get in my way?" he barked.

"No, sir."

"Then go! I'm busy here!" snapped Theudas.

Theudas then saw where the stranger had been stroking the stone's grey porous surface. An unusual splotch of dark red—what appeared to be freshly dried blood—was smeared on the inner edge of the stone press.

"What do you know about that?" quizzed Theudas.

"I don't know what you mean," the stranger squirmed.

Liar!

"Right here. Tell me. What happened . . . here!" Theudas pointed to the spot.

"I have no idea what you're talking about."

"Don't be stupid. Someone got hurt here," said Theudas. "Someone who didn't belong here!"

"Please, I just came to remember—"

"Remember what? What did you forget? Tell me. We'll find it quickly. Then you can leave!"

"It's just that—"

"Who are you, anyway? What's your business here?"

"My name is Peter and . . ." His voice faltered.

For a moment, Theudas didn't make the connection; then his eyes widened with the realization of who the stranger was.

Hold onto him, he told himself. *There could be a bounty on his head. I could get a new mule out of this stroke of good luck.*

Rubbing his beard, Theudas relished the possibilities. "You're one of the followers of the Rabbi. No?"

"No! I mean, yes," faltered Peter. Conflicting emotions were at war within him once again, as they had been two nights before.

"I hear they've been looking for you," said Theudas.

A sense of panic was beginning to overrun what little fortification remained in Peter's mind.

He stuttered, "I just, uh . . ." Peter started moving away. "I've just got to go!" He then spun around and fled into the dense grove, staggering around one tree and then another until he was out of view.

138

"WHY PEOPLE are so upset over the Rabbi," smirked Theudas, talking to his mule, "I'll never understand."

Theudas scratched his head. His donkey stood motionless, awaiting its next order.

"You dusty old jack. Someday, they'll have to cut your dead carcass away from this harness—maybe even bury the two of us together."

Lifting the heavy basket over the edge of the large stone basin, he then poured the olive berries into its base. They were the characteristic dull yellowish-green color. Some were slightly bruised from having lain on the ground overnight.

"If you ask me, all that nonsense is a waste of time and money," Theudas reasoned with the mule, scraping the olives down to the bottom of the circular basin with the wooden paddle. "Had Miriam held onto the money that she gave to the Rabbi, I could've traded you in for a new and stronger ass by now."

Tossing the paddle aside, Theudas then walked to the right side of the mule. With the familiar pat on the rump and a spirited "Yip," Theudas and his old mule began their monotonous ritual of plodding around the millstone.

This particular task could not be hurried. Usually the work in the grove was leisurely anyhow. Olive trees were slow-growing trees, requiring years of patient labor until they became fruit-bearing. As such, the trees came to symbolize the values of settlement and peace. In just one day, a hostile army could destroy what had taken generations to cultivate.

In truth, the crushing of the olives was really just a small part of Theudas' job. The trees required attention year-round. Frequently, the soil had to be plowed and broken up so that rainwater could reach the trees' roots. Occasionally Theudas would mulch *chuwwarah* (a type of fertilizer) into the soil to enrich it.

Today's chores, however, were limited mostly to the stone

press. With each lap around the central pivot, the hard stony kernels and meaty part of the olives were cracked and crushed. Under the grinding weight, each pass of the heavy stone caused the sharp snapping sounds to yield to the dull, quaggy sounds indicative of the olives' now mushy consistency.

SURROUNDING THE milling station were trees, young and old, of the olive yard. Their produce hung generously from some trees and sparsely from others. The stiff leaves were a dull grey-green, frosted with silver.

Near the edge of the grove, just inside the stone wall, was a cluster of the oldest trees—their trunks and branches twisted and gnarled—three of which were naturally hollowed out at their knotty bases. Someday these trees would lose their strength to produce fruit and would be cut down. They would be used for carpentry wood or burned for fuel.

Sheltered from the sun, under the leafy canopy of an older tree near the perimeter of the grove, Peter hunched against the stone wall. His body twitched with fatigue. He desperately needed to rest, but closing his eyes only invited an endless re-play of the horrific scene from two nights before.

Here in this same grove, a place normally serene and peaceful at night, was where the upheaval began. The temple guards, led by Judas, shattered the evening calm. There was a kiss of betrayal. Then came a skirmish that left a servant's ear detached. Then the Teacher was arrested and led away.

I'm a coward! lamented Peter.

Peter picked up a rock that fit easily in his right fist. Despondently, he first examined the rock and then gazed out at the sky above.

I'm to blame!

Pain exploded in his right thigh as the edge of the rock smashed against his flesh. Once . . . twice . . . and again, he hammered the rock against himself. It was dull enough not to

140

break the skin but sharp enough, with the knifing thrust of his arm, to quickly crush the blood vessels below the skin and begin severe bruising.

He was counting on me, Peter pounded. *This reproach is upon me.*

The blows, while painful, also felt good to Peter. It was his punishment. It was what he deserved. Mutilation of the flesh was the first step in the chastisement of his soul. Only after some penalty was paid (any penalty!) would relief come and a measure of rest be earned.

You could've stepped in, he berated himself. *This didn't have to happen this way.*

Sequestered in his anguish, Peter then thrust the stone against his left upper arm, against his bicep.

If only I'd been braver. If only I'd taken a stand. Instead, I claimed I never knew Him.

He pounded harder.

Peter, you dog! You said, "No, not me"—and that to a servant girl. What were you thinking?

Exhausted, Peter slumped to the ground and laid on his side, the rough soil against his face. His tired grip eventually loosened and the rock toppled to the ground. His chest convulsed, every breath competing with his anguished cries.

Oh, God, you were counting on me and I failed you! Wasn't it just two years ago when the Master asked, "But whom say ye that I am?"

Indeed, it had been just two short years since Jesus asked that question. Peter's answer was already legendary: "Thou art the Christ, the Son of the living God." It was a defining moment, not just in Jesus' ministry but also in Peter's role among the disciples.

Peter continued in his self-incrimination. *You idiot! You knew the truth! No one else knew it, or at least no one else had the courage to risk being wrong. The others faltered—afraid to tell*

Him what they themselves thought. But you, Peter, you spoke up! And you were right! He was the Anointed One, the Son of the living God!

Surveying the trees, Peter cried out, "Yahweh God, what has happened? What went wrong? The Messiah wasn't supposed to die. I thought that the Anointed One couldn't be touched. Was I wrong? Was all this just a delusion? What have I missed? God, I'm not sure I know who You are now, or who Jesus was. I don't even know who I am anymore!"

Peter lay motionless in the deep shadows of the trees, reflecting on all that the Master had said to him. Two years before, the Master had affirmed him in front of all the disciples and had given him the Aramaic nickname *Cephas*, which corresponded to the Greek *Petros*, or Peter, meaning "a rock."

Peter scoffed at himself. *Peter, the rock? Solid? Sturdy? Unmovable? Me? I'm a rock, all right: Hard-headed! Cut off from Him who is the living Rock!*

He shook his head cynically.

My name is still Simon. That was my name before I ever knew the Master, and that's who I have become again!

Peter then cried aloud in prayer, "Jesus wasn't supposed to die. Do You see me, God? Do You even care? Look at me—I'm dying down here! My soul is being cracked and crushed like those cursed olives—and for what purpose? Jesus wasn't supposed to die. That's not the way it was supposed to end!"

AFTER THE olive berries were thoroughly cracked and crushed, Theudas scrapped the crushed meats and kernels toward the basin's edge and scooped it all into large sackcloth bags. The mesh fabric of the coarse bags served to strain the oil from the soft pulp of the olives.

Glancing over his shoulder, Theudas noticed that there was another intruder in the orchard now. He sighed inwardly, his patience wearing thin.

142

From where Peter lay, he couldn't tell whether the person approaching the milling station was a young man or just a boy. Soon he saw that it was the owner's son. Marcus was like his deceased father in the way he conducted business. He believed that making a profit was more important than anything. Like his father, Marcus was apt to drive away an annoying passerby. Only when Miriam stopped by did he or Theudas feign hospitality.

Peter watched the old man and the young fellow talk. Theudas pointed toward the edge of the grove. After a few minutes, he patted the owner's son on the shoulder and returned to his work. Marcus walked off in the opposite direction from where Peter had been spying.

At the milling station, Theudas continued in his labors. The sackcloth bags, now filled with their crushed yellowish-green mush, were placed on a large, flat stone which had a series of shallow grooves running out from its center. With the sacks laid as flat as possible, Theudas then put his foot on a wooden lever that lowered a heavy, flat stone onto its base—pressing the mashed olive berries beneath it. The pressure of the weight forced the oil from the olives to ooze out through the mesh and be channeled down into a large cavity at the base of the press.

Some orchards specialized in growing olives just for consumption. These green and black olives were picked when they were quite ripe and pickled in a briny solution and later eaten with bread. The olives from Miriam's grove, however, were used for oil—as medicine for wounds, as seasoning for meals and even as fuel for the evening lamps of surrounding neighborhoods. The greasy substance pressed out of the berries was called "shemen," or "beaten oil," and would later be taken by Theudas into Jerusalem to be sold.

In Jewish tradition, the oil from the olive berries had great symbolic value. As far back as Noah, it had been an emblem of peace and blessing, of joy and prosperity, of the presence and power of Yahweh God Himself.

Theudas sat in the shadow of the milling station, waiting for the compression to slowly extract its prize; Peter lay in the shadows of the grove, agonizing under the compression of his own grief. Pangs of hunger rumbled through his stomach. The temptation to pick and eat from the bounty of olives around him was contested by the greater need to remain hidden, at least until Theudas had left for the evening.

Trying to console himself, Peter thought back to passages of Scripture that he had committed to memory: Purge me with hyssop and I shall be clean, wash me and I shall be whiter than snow. Make me hear joy and gladness, that the bones you have broken may rejoice. Hide Your face from my sins, and blot out all my iniquities. Create in me a clean heart O God and renew a steadfast spirit within me. Do not cast me away from Your presence . . .

Nevertheless, as Peter reached heavenward to alleviate his shame, voices of condemnation echoed in his mind: "You didn't produce any fruit, but I was patient," they faintly whispered. "I dug around you. I fertilized you. I kept you growing. And after awhile, I looked. There was still no fruit, so I cut you down . . . down . . . down . . ."

The dreamlike voices continued to haunt him, drifting out from the shadowy hollows of the gnarled old trees. "Down . . . down . . . down . . ."

FOURTEEN

WHAT SEEMED like just minutes had really been two hours when Peter awoke from a fitful sleep. The sun had set and the milling station was quiet. Now, it was finally safe for Peter to walk about.

Theudas had gone home after the oil from the press had been extracted. All that remained were the flattened sackcloth bags under the heavy stone, filled with their pulpy waste. For Peter, it was a symbol of his own emptiness. Anything good that was in him had been crushed and pressed out by everything that had happened in the last two days.

Peter would have lingered there all night in the pale moonlight, but he suddenly heard footsteps. Swiftly, he dashed back toward the trees, fearing the wrath of the temple guards.

They've returned . . . to finish what they started, he thought. *To arrest and condemn. To crucify and kill.*

Nearing the canopy of trees, Peter stumbled on the uneven surface of the rocky garden. His right ankle twisted, sending a fiery bolt of pain up his leg, radiating through his hip. With nothing to grab onto, Peter fell to his knees, catching himself with the palms of his hands on the ground. The pain was so intense it made him feel queasy. He was afraid he might vomit, but there was no time to wallow in his misery.

Get up, he ordered himself. *Hurry! You're almost there. Get to the cover of the trees. Now!*

Crawling on hands and knees, Peter dragged himself away

145

from the millstone clearing, over an old stump, and into the trees. As his belly scraped against the stump, the faint voice that had taunted him earlier returned.

You didn't produce any fruit, but I was patient. And after awhile, I looked. There was still no fruit, so I cut you down . .

Looking back at the stump, Peter moaned, *That's me. Nothing to show for my life. Cut down!*

As Peter examined the stump more closely, however, he noticed that a small green shoot sprouted from it. It wasn't unusual for new shoots to spring forth from old stumps. After a few years, the shoots would grow into new trees that would eventually produce a bounty of fruit.

As Peter examined the little shoot, a voice of prophetic hope, not condemnation, now whispered: *Behold a new shoot will come out of the stump of Jesse and will become a new tree.*

"Peter? Is that you?"

Peter froze.

It was a gentle, feminine voice, not the voice of a rough soldier or temple guard. It was a voice of charity, not contempt.

Still, his mind raced with fear. His hands again clawed at the dirt.

"Peter, stop! It's all right. It's just us."

It was Thaddaeus, Magdalene, and Mary.

Thaddaeus was the first to crouch near the terrorized disciple. Peter's swollen eyes shifted frantically, darting to avoid visual contact with the others. Each of his friends, however, caught the wild look of distrust.

"It's over," Peter whimpered. "I am so sorry. I'm a reproach."

"Shhh, Peter," said Thaddaeus calmly. "Of course you're hurting. We're all hurting right now. It just seems so unbelievable that Jesus is gone."

"You don't understand," cried Peter. "It's my fault that He's gone!"

"No, it's not," assured Thaddaeus. "Just come home with us—we've been looking everywhere for you. It's safer there."

"Don't you understand?" Peter now pulled back, resisting the care of his friends. "I can't go home. I let the Master down. I failed Him!"

"What do you mean?"

Peter wailed, "I denied Him. I claimed I never knew Him. It happened three times earlier and once again this afternoon. If only I had done something different, He might still be alive!"

Thaddaeus countered, "We don't know that, Peter."

"Just come home with us," Magdalene pleaded.

"I can't. What am I supposed to say to the others? That I denied my best friend?" Peter cried. "That when I had a chance to stop the madness, I just caved in and let Him die?"

Peter then erupted into heaving sobs. He was physically trembling under the weight of his sorrow. For the next hour, his friends encircled him with their love, sharing the depth of his grief, whispering prayers over him, and embracing their friend.

Slowly, Peter began to rise from his state of despair. His cathartic wailing quieted to a low moaning.

When his trembling abated, Peter summoned the courage to look up at his friends.

"Oh, Mary," Peter's eyes reached for the mother and then away.

Without hesitation, Mary gently took Peter by the shoulders and pulled his head close to hers. Through her tears, she whispered, "Peter, you were always like a son to me. I've lost one son. I will not lose another."

The words were a soothing balm, massaging his soul. Stiff

from sitting, Mary then shifted her weight to kneel next to Peter. She slowly lifted his chin in her hand.

"Look at me, Peter."

Shame was losing its grip on the disciple.

As he slowly lifted his gaze, Mary said tenderly, "Each of us is hurting, too. Perhaps we're all to blame."

While the eyes of Mary softly gleamed with compassion and forbearance, they also betrayed her personal anguish and exhaustion from the past two days.

"I'm not angry with you," she reassured him. "And I refuse to let you carry this burden alone."

Mary then rose. Stooping over, she gently pulled Peter to his feet.

"Please, come home," she said.

Peter hesitated.

"Oh, don't be a mule about it," she said. "It's cold out here and my legs are cramping!"

Peter caught her wink. His whole body seemed to sag with relief.

With a smile, Mary added, "Besides, your supper is waiting! Now let's go!"

On the foot that didn't hurt, Peter first hopped gingerly. He then reached for the supportive arm of Thaddaeus, who served as his crutch.

Nodding to Mary, he signaled his acceptance of her mercy. With the aid of his friends, accompanied by the pain of both a swollen ankle and a sorrowful heart, Peter began hobbling from his Gethsemane.

FIFTEEN

IRIAM JERKED awake as the dirt floor and adobe walls shook violently from yet another earthquake. Dust seeped down through the compacted clay ceiling. On the shelves, earthenware vibrated. She first staggered and then crawled on all fours to a nearby table, balancing precariously on the ever-shifting floor. Before long, the tremors subsided.

Although it was still mostly dark outside, the predawn light had already begun to inch up over the horizon. Miriam would have returned to her bed to sleep a little longer, but she heard the footsteps of the disciples scurrying about on the roof above. Go back to bed, you oafs! she almost yelled out. But out of consideration for Mary, who somehow managed to sleep through the quake, she restrained herself.

As she straightened up the downstairs, Miriam reflected on the night before. It had been late when they had finally gotten Peter safely back to her house. After a quick supper and the comfort of a cold ankle compress, Peter was helped upstairs by Matthew and John, where he promptly dozed off. Miriam made it unmistakably clear to the other disciples that Peter needed his rest, and that she expected complete silence, unlike the previous night.

Miriam, Magdalene and John agreed that early the next morning, they would take Peter with them to check on the tomb of Jesus. While it would have been better for Peter to

149

stay off his sore ankle for a day or two, Miriam didn't trust the other disciples. The last few days had been volatile and, for now, the others were still unaware of why Peter had gone missing.

For a time, Miriam would look out for Peter just as she had the Lord's mother. She surmised that someday, when everyone reflected back on this dark period, they would undoubtedly fault Peter and Judas as being the two who had failed the most. In truth, however, just about every follower had let their Lord down in some way or another. But it would be easier to cast stones at someone else, than to admit one's own shortcomings.

Eventually Magdalene stumbled in from the other room, rubbed the sleep from her eyes, and helped Miriam with the cleaning. A short time later, Magdalene called Miriam over to the window. Gazing out, the women drank in the most beautiful time of day in Jerusalem—daybreak over the eastern horizon. A weather front had moved through earlier, and dark purple clouds vividly swelled with crimson-edged billows. Lively orangish-yellow shafts of morning light pierced the predawn sky.

As the two marveled at the Creator's hand that canvassed the heavens, the serenity of the morning was again shattered when two of the disciples bumbled noisily down the outside stairs. It was Andrew and Thaddaeus.

"Go back to bed!" Miriam scolded. "It's not time to get up yet." Actually, it was time to be up. Miriam was just weary from all the company. She wanted them to stay in bed and out of the way for a few hours longer.

"We're leaving," said Thaddaeus.

Miriam breathed an inward sigh of relief.

"Already?" She feigned disappointment "Where are you going?"

"To Emmaus," said Andrew. "It's Thaddaeus' hometown."

Emmaus was located three-score furlongs from Jerusalem,

about seven miles northwest. The village was noted for its therapeutic hot springs. Thaddaeus assured Andrew that going there would be restful. Travel restrictions both in and out of Jerusalem appeared to have eased, and getting away would be good for them both. Two lesser-known followers, Cleopas and Alphaeus, were to meet up with them there.

Miriam said, "We're going to the garden tomb this morning. It's on your way. Why don't you come with us?"

While Miriam would have preferred to journey to the Lord's grave with just John, Magdalene, and Peter, she was concerned about how they would roll the huge stone away from the tomb's entrance, assuming the guards would even permit it. The final application of aromatic myrrh and spices two nights before had been cut short. Even with the help of the soldiers, a few extra hands might be helpful.

Just then, Peter and John came stumbling down from the roof.

"Why is everyone awake down here?" complained John. "Does no one sleep?"

"Shhh! Mary's still asleep," said Miriam. "She's had difficulty resting. Let's not wake her."

As quickly as she could, Miriam hurried everyone out of the house to go visit the tomb. Outside, they waited as John ascended the stairs to tell the remaining disciples to stay there and watch over Mary.

Once John came back down, the two women and four disciples departed and traveled northward through the Upper City. The narrow streets throughout the Mishneh district were mostly deserted. A few merchants bustled about, preparing to reopen their shops on this morning after the Sabbath.

"Just how are we going to convince the soldiers to open the tomb?" asked John

"They'll just have to," said Miriam. "We weren't finished the other night and they knew it. I told them we'd return."

PRISON BOOK PROJECT
P.O. Box 1146
Sharpes, FL 32959

"And what if they refuse?" asked John.

"Perhaps they might respond to a little feminine charm," suggested Magdalene, flipping her hair and casting a kiss.

Thaddaeus bantered, "I didn't think Miriam had any charm."

Andrew burst out laughing.

"I heard that!" Miriam said as she slapped Thaddaeus' arm.

Magdalene and the other disciples chuckled as Thaddaeus playfully cowered from Miriam, pretending to be hurt.

The solemnity of the past few days had been wearisome. A moment of laughter was good medicine for them all. Onward through the Tyropoeon Valley and out through the Fish Gate they strolled.

APPROACHING THE gated cemetery, their moods became more sober. Entering the garden, they slowly, cautiously approached the area of the tomb, with Peter and John in the lead.

The men stopped short. Something was terribly wrong.

"The guards!" John bellowed. "Where are the guards?"

When they had left the grave two nights before, it was under the watch of the most disciplined of soldiers. These soldiers were fierce warriors. To desert their watch would be treasonous and punishable by death.

Closer now, the group collectively gasped at the sight of the tomb's entrance. The opening to the dark tunnel was exposed.

A distance away from the cave lay the huge blocking stone. It was not rolled carefully to the side and wedged uphill in its channel; rather, it appeared as though it had been forcibly heaved outward and away from the tomb itself.

"They've taken Him!" shrieked Magdalene. "They've taken Him away!"

"Grave robbers?" asked John.

"There's no way it could be grave robbers," said Thaddaeus. "The military regiment would have been impenetrable to common thieves."

Quickly running ahead, John was the first one to reach the cave. Timidly, he peeked inside.

Right behind him, walking slower because of his injured ankle, Peter circled around John and practically lunged right into the tomb.

There was no corpse!

Peter called to Miriam, "Come up—you've got to see this!"

As Miriam hiked to the entrance, Peter asked, "Are you sure this is the tomb where you laid Him?"

"Of course it is!" said Miriam.

As she crawled through the entrance, she expected to see the grave-bands strewn about from the heist of the corpse. Instead, a hollow, almost deflated shell of bands and fabric that once enshrouded the torso lay neatly on the ledge. Against the far end of the rock shelf lay the face-bands.

Peter was flabbergasted.

"Something's not right here!" said Miriam.

The condition of the grave-clothes, and the stone's position, were indeed odd. This was not a scene where military guards had been overpowered and a grave hastily pillaged.

"They've taken Him!" Miriam said angrily, emerging from the tomb. "I can't believe it. They've taken Him away!"

"Who took Him?" Magdalene asked.

"Who do you think?" fumed Miriam. "Pilate and the temple guards, of course!"

"But where?" John asked.

"Where?" scolded Miriam. "The first question is, 'Why?' Why did they take Him? And why didn't they have the decency to forewarn His mother?"

"We've got to tell Mary!" said Peter.

Miriam nodded. "Then we'll march right over to the procurator and find out what is going on."

"Do you need us to stay behind?" asked Andrew.

John could see that Thaddaeus and Andrew looked as weary as everyone else. Although their help with the procurator might be needed, it would be better to keep them from harm, if there was any danger.

"Go on your way," John urged.

Miriam quickly raised a hand of protest.

"Go! Leave town," John said firmly, batting away her objection, "and send our greetings to Cleopas, Alphaeus and to the rest of our friends in Emmaus."

The remaining four departed from the tomb and walked back toward the gated entrance of the garden. Off in the distance, they could see Andrew and Thaddaeus hurrying northward on the road toward Emmaus.

"You all go," said Magdalene. "I'll stay here."

"But you need to come with us," said Peter. "It's important we stay together."

"I'm not ready to leave," she said. "Not just yet."

SIXTEEN

I N HER anguish, sitting next to the hollow entrance of the tomb, Magdalene recalled the poetic words of David the great king: For in death there is no remembrance of thee: in the grave who shall give thee thanks?

First, they arrested Jesus without warning. Then, they crucified Him. Now, they had stolen His body.

Not once did she have a moment to say goodbye. He was snatched from her as if He never existed, as if the memory of Him was never meant to be.

Not only was Magdalene frustrated with the enemies of Jesus, she was also angered by His friends. Although she didn't say anything, Magdalene had felt disheartened two nights before as she assisted in the burial preparations. It seemed that everything at the cross and the tomb was so abuzz with activity that any chance for solitude and quiet reflection was lost. The well-meaning but intrusive spectators, along with the assorted religious leaders and guards, were all impinging on the personal closure she felt she deserved but was never afforded.

Finally, a quiet moment! she thought, as her three friends now made their way back to Jerusalem. Even with the unexpected removal of the corpse, there was now something strangely peaceful about this cemetery. Facing the cave and seated with her back resting against the blocking stone, a cool breeze in her hair, Magdalene closed her eyes and drifted from the horror of the last two days to a better world—daydreaming about her Lord.

In the few short months since her deliverance, she had felt freer in her spirit than ever before. In His presence, she felt the acceptance and love she had always longed for since she was a little girl.

In her childhood, Magdalene's mother and father had died unexpectedly. When her aunt and uncle took custody of her, she was forced to leave everything that was familiar. It was then that her innocence came unraveled. When her protectors were absent, her virtue was stolen by an older cousin who fondled and raped her. The molestation spanned an eight-year period.

To survive, Magdalene allowed her mind to regress during the threats and intimidation to the point where she mentally withdrew from the realities of the world around her. Trust and self-confidence were supplanted by trepidation and self-hatred. Now in the garden cemetery, Magdalene felt herself beginning to withdraw again.

It's happening. Please . . . no . . . not again! Her will furiously rowed against the current of relapse.

The tomb had been raped and pillaged, as her life had once been. Her Lord was the first to love her in a way that resembled the father's love she once embraced. Now, just as her father was suddenly taken away from her, the Lord was stripped from her as well. He was gone.

I'm slipping, she moaned.

Once again, Magdalene felt orphaned. The Father's love was gone. Virtue and innocence were again plundered.

"Oh, God. Please . . . You must help me!"

A STIRRING amidst the trees caught Magdalene's attention and snapped her back to reality. The soldiers. They've returned. Have they come to make more arrests?

Hidden behind the large blocking stone, Magdalene turned and crouched down.

When she peeked around the stone, she saw that it was—

Marcus? What is he doing here?

Indeed it was Marcus. He was loitering in the trees, discovered, once again, in a place he didn't belong. Just when Magdalene finally had a private moment, this new intruder arrived.

Isn't this wonderful! she thought sarcastically. Of all people, why did it have to be Marcus?

"Marcus!" she scolded, popping up from behind the stone. "There you go again, sneaking around. . ."

"I am not!" he replied defiantly.

"But you're not where you're supposed to be, are you?"

"And just where am I supposed to be?"

"Marcus, anywhere but here is where you're supposed to be!" said Magdalene, her jaw squarely set. Although an angry tear rolled down her cheek, she continued to glare at Marcus, silently willing him to leave her alone.

"Why are you crying?" Marcus asked, curious.

"Just leave me alone!" she replied.

"Tell me, Magdalene—what's wrong?"

"You know what's wrong," she responded angrily. "Pilate has taken the body of Jesus."

For a moment, Marcus almost seemed as if he was going to respond sympathetically to the weeping woman. But then he shrugged, indifferently.

"What does it matter? He's dead already."

Magdalene was shocked by his callousness.

"Marcus!" she exploded. His hard-heartedness was beyond belief.

"Just go away! Leave me alone!" she cried, sinking to her knees.

She was surprised when Marcus knelt next to her, regret in

his eyes. She knew that, in his own immature way, he really did care for her.

But when he tried to embrace her, his touch was as abhorrent as the molesting hands of the cousin she once knew.

She quickly pulled back and pushed him away.

"Go away!" she cried. "You don't care about my feelings."

"Yes, I do," Marcus countered. But there was a hardness to his countenance again.

"No, you don't, Marcus! Thomas told me last night what you had said to him, about throwing your voice."

"I have no idea—"

"You're a liar!" she railed, staring him down.

She continued. "Jesus delivered me! I know I'm free! Your stupid voices and teasing have held me back. Do you hear me, Marcus? They've held me back. You've hurt me!"

Shaking her head, she walked slowly backward, away from him.

"Now go! Leave me alone!" she screamed. "I hate you!"

At her words, Marcus snapped.

"Magdalene, you think you're so perfect, don't you. But you're actually stupid and gullible," he sneered. "It's me who's the clever one!"

Then he threw his head back and began to laugh.

Magdalene had considered running away, but now she was too angry. Knowing that she was still thinking clearly and under control, she stood unflinching against his verbal attack.

"You're not clever, Marcus—you're nothing but a fool!" With that, she slapped him across the face.

Furious now, Marcus cocked his fist, ready to punch her.

She tilted her head defiantly, unafraid, daring him to try and hit her.

Something about the way she was looking at him caused Marcus to slowly lower his fist. He spit on the ground at her feet.

"You're the one who is a fool," Marcus said, trying to get in one last jab. "You did believe the voices were real! Even Peter and the guards believed it!"

He spun around and started walking away. But then he stopped and turned to face Magdalene one more time.

"The devil knows even Judas was duped!" he snarled.

IN THAT awful moment of disclosure, purity magnified impurity. Even from a distance, Marcus could see Magdalene's eyes—eyes that remained fixed on him. Those brown, almond-shaped eyes which, amazingly, overflowed with compassion. Even when she was angry, her eyes still reflected a deep kindness and purity of spirit. They only served to magnify Marcus' confusion all the more.

So many times his own mother had quoted from the wisdom books, *He that winketh with the eye causeth sorrow: but a prating fool shall fall.* Before Magdalene even had a chance to question him about Judas, Marcus turned and fled from her presence.

She's right! What a thick-skulled fool I've been, Marcus berated himself desperately, as he ran.

What was I thinking back there? Why did I say all that? Magdalene will never like me now!

It was over. He would run away from his love. He would run as far as possible, to escape his own madness.

Maybe I'm the fool, after all—hoping that someone like Magdalene would love me.

Wrenching away from the furious young woman, Marcus bolted out of the garden cemetery. Leaping across the stone ridge and hightailing it through the dense brush and tall weeds, the gangly young man was pitted against himself in a race for sanity.

His outburst against the maiden had hastened what was certain to be the final act of his life's sordid drama. Just mo-

159

ments before, in her presence, the curtain that had hidden his immaturity abruptly lifted, and the self-absorption, greed and loneliness that had engulfed him since his father's death took center stage.

Hurdling a fallen log, Marcus thought that the only thing that could possibly slow him down would be the sight of the slender young woman herself, chasing after him. He imagined that she might still care. She could help him. She could pity him.

Still running hard, Marcus shot a glance behind him, hoping. . .

SMACK!

Marcus fell to the ground as the pain exploded in his head.

A fleeting glimpse of something bright and spirited and a faint, seraphic chord yielded to a halo of darkness and a loud, endless clang that pulsated in his head.

Slipping quickly, his mind flooded with faint memories of mourning and madness. Images that had come to define his life endlessly replayed in those last murky moments of consciousness.

Darkness pressed in. Marcus was too weak to fight back. The blackness of oblivion took one last swallow as purplish-red blossoms danced and drifted down from above. . .

THE COLLISION had knocked him unconscious. Exactly how long he was out, he didn't know.

Lying on the ground, still dazed, Marcus struggled to lift his head. A dull throb pounded within. Rubbing his eyes, Marcus quickly shook his head, trying to clear his mind.

Rolling over, Marcus slowly regained his bearings. He looked around to find out who or what had hit him. No one was nearby. He was still alone.

As his vision cleared, he realized what he had crashed into. In his wild desperation to flee the cemetery, he hadn't been looking where he was going. Taking that last glance backward, he had run headlong into one of the garden trees.

Lying back on the ground, rubbing his temples, he gazed up. The collision had sent a few of the tree's purple-red blossoms dancing and drifting downward from the impact.

Of all trees, Marcus sighed. *A redbud.*

The tree was slightly smaller than the one he'd seen at the Hinnom ridge but solid nonetheless. As Marcus struggled to gather his wits, tiny blossoms floated down, like tears. Just as they had for Judas.

Closing his eyes, the imagery and sounds of the strangulation again vividly flooded his mind. Ever since he'd secretly followed Judas, Marcus couldn't free his head from the horrible memories of the suicide.

"Please, just make it go away," he had prayed.

But whenever he closed his eyes and tried to sleep, the haunting images were still there. He couldn't escape them.

For the first time, Marcus felt truly guilty and ashamed about his antics. Only a day earlier, he had bragged to Thomas about how he'd learned the soothsayer's art of speaking from the hollow of one's belly. Perhaps this practice was forbidden not only because it distracted God's people from fully trusting in Him, but also because it required those who would deceive to speak from the hollow of their soul. And to speak from a hollowed soul was to be deceived themselves.

"This isn't what I wanted!" he cried aloud.

After his father had died, his mother was so caught up in her grief. He only wanted to be loved. As he grew older, he increasingly longed for affirmation and a sense of significance. By manipulating and exploiting others, as devious as it was, he finally felt some sense of control. Yet, in this moment of self-revelation, the veil was finally lifted, exposing his utter abasement and powerlessness to control anything.

From somewhere nearby, Marcus now heard a faint

whisper. It was a muffled exhortation, a hollow murmur, not unlike that which he had conjured up so many times before: *There was no fruit, so I cut you down . . .*

It seemed to be an audible voice this time. Marcus gasped. Spinning around, he looked wildly about.

"Who's there?" he called out. But no one was there.

He trembled.

The echo drummed on in his mind: *Down . . . down . . . down . . .*

Marcus held his head. It throbbed relentlessly.

The whisper was real. It was devilish. This was no prank.

What's happening to me?

"GET . . . OUT . . . OF . . . MY . . . HEAD!" he screamed breathlessly. "Please, God, oh please!" Marcus begged. "I'm not ready. Please don't let this happen!"

Harnessing every bit of strength that he'd ever wasted on wrongdoing, Marcus fought against the voice in his mind.

No, this is not the end! His mother had found hope and he, too, would now find it.

No, this will not be my end! Although his father had died, Marcus refused to let despair steal away his own good memories and hope for a future.

"No!" he shouted. "I . . . WILL . . . LIVE!"

He collapsed to the ground, gasping for air.

MARCUS' MIND SLOWLY cleared. He thought about the cemetery he had fled from. So many questions swirled in his mind, as they did in the minds of the others who had discovered the empty tomb. There was more to that garden grave than he would ever understand.

The Teacher has died—but how could mere humans steal away one who is the Son of God, if He is who He claimed to be? And what about the guards? How could grave robbers get past them? And the grave clothes—how did the thieves pull the body out of them without disturbing the swaddling bands? It's almost like He had melted, or slithered, out of them. And what about the stone? It wasn't just rolled away. It was cast away from the entrance as if it were a mere pebble in the hands of an all-powerful God.

An all-powerful God. Something sparked inside Marcus. *I see it!*

With godly contrition, he began to pray. When he was younger, he would recite the scripted prayers that his father and mother had set before him. Such prayers reflected the rich heritage of his parent's religion. But in this moment of self-revelation, Marcus cried out passionately to God as if He was really there and ready to be known.

"God, I've been such a fool," he whispered. "Just as the blocking stone has been removed to reveal the empty tomb, You've now removed the stone from my eyes. I see my emptiness. Somehow, some way, fill the hollow of my—"

A HIGH-pitched shriek suddenly pierced the stillness of the morning, interrupting the expunging prayer of Marcus. It was the cry of a woman.

Marcus quickly turned to listen.

Magdalene! It came from where Marcus had left Magdalene.

The soldiers! They're back! They've got Magdalene. She needs my help!

Marcus leapt to his feet and and ran back toward the ridge.

Closer, but still far from her sight, Marcus again heard her cry out.

"Go away, Marcus!" the voice yelled. "I told you to leave me alone."

Marcus stopped in his tracks, taken aback.

Who is she talking to?

He was nowhere near Magdalene. He was still on the far

edge of the ridge that formed the western side of the burial cave, well out of her view.

Maybe she really is crazy, he thought, concerned now. *Maybe she really does hear voices.*

From near the top of the burial cave, Marcus heard Magdalene sobbing, still uttering something unintelligible. She sounded afraid and confused. She must be in trouble. He had to move—quickly! This was his chance to rescue her—to really be her hero! But what if he wasn't welcome? What if she didn't want to see him? Hadn't he just fled from her, bewildered and ashamed?

Then Marcus heard her gasp, "Rabbi!"

Still apprehensive, Marcus crawled on hands and knees, inching forward on the ridge, being careful not to be seen. Then he peered over.

What he saw left him speechless. Still hidden from view, Marcus could now see everything clearly. A pure white light radiated from below. It was the most astonishing thing he had ever witnessed, a scene of undiluted glory. This was no apparition or soothsaying divination. This was indisputably real!

With every fiber of his being alive now, Marcus scooted down from the edge and off the backside of the burial cave. He then sprinted through the garden gate in a race to catch up with Miriam, Peter, and John.

"I've got to tell them!" he laughed. "They won't believe this."

He could barely believe it himself.

It can't be real. But it is!

As Marcus ran, he knew that his burst of happiness was not merely transient, as if rattling loosely in a hollow clay jar. Heaven's joy was genuinely settling in. Virtue was being absorbed and finding lodging in his soul. His spirit was engaged. Love had found a home.

Marcus then slowed his pace.

Although panting and breathless, he felt oddly refreshed and invigorated. His spirit was renewed.

Marcus stopped. Bending over to catch his breath, he started chuckling. The longer he thought, the harder he laughed. Before long, tears of laughter rolled down his cheeks.

Of course, he wanted to be the first to tell them. News like this would be absolutely riveting. But for the first time, he didn't have to be first.

"I'll let Magdalene tell it," Marcus said, smiling. "She can be the first. This is her moment. This is her story."

Now when Jesus was risen early the first day of the week, He appeared first to Mary Magdalene . . . And she went and told them that she had been with Him (Mark 16:9-10)

ABOUT THE AUTHOR

Brian J. Buriff is a pastor and has authored two other books, *Serenity for the Soul* and *Revelations to Go!* He is a graduate of Anderson University and Luther Rice Seminary, holding a Master of Divinity and a Master of Arts in Counseling degree. He and his wife Amber and their two sons reside in the greater Cincinnati, Ohio area.

To contact the author for speaking engagements, write:

Brian J. Buriff
P.O. Box 181401
Fairfield, OH 45018-1401

Or visit online at www.BrianBuriff.com
or www.BeyondThePassion-TheNovel.com